# House with a Heart

by

## Rick Iekel

## DEDICATION

*This story is dedicated to the memory of my brother, Robert Iekel, who died of polio at the age of nine, only two years after we moved to the farm. I was four at the time of his death. Just as I imagine sweet little Sarah might have been, back in 1855, I am told Bob was a kind and gentle soul, good-tempered, generous and true to his family's values. Like Sarah, his death was sudden and tragic, his loss immense for both parents and siblings.*

*May he rest in peace, along with Sarah W. in the arms of a living God.*

## The Town of Ashford
### (Gazeteer of the State of New York – 1860)

**ASHFORD** – was formed from Ellicottville, Feb. 16, 1824. It is centrally located on the N. border of the co. The surface is hilly, with ridges extending generally in a N. and S. direction. The highest points in the N. part are 300 feet above the valleys. Cattaraugus Creek, forming the N. boundary, and Buttermilk Creek are the principal streams. The soil is a slaty loam intermixwd with gravel and clay. Maple sugar is largely manufactured. **Ashford,** (p.v.) in the s.w. part of the town, contains a grist and saw mill, 2 churches, and 86 dwellings; **East Ashford** (p.o.) contains 9 churches and 11 dwellings. The first settlers were Henry Frank and his two sons, Andrew and Jacob H., from Herkimer co., who located on Lot 56, in 1816. The first church (F.W.Bap.) was organized in 1821, by Elder Richard M. Cary. There are now 6 churches in town.

# Town of Ashford - 1856

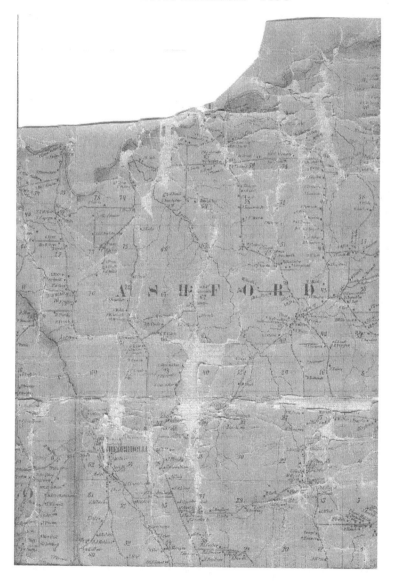

## Acknowledgements

Among items found when my father moved to senior housing were papers tracing the ownership of my childhood home back to its beginning in 1854. I've often wondered, "Who were those people?" Thus began a journey that gave birth to this story.

Michael and Sarah (last name withheld for privacy) were real people. A down-to-earth pioneer farmer, Michael apparently had neither time nor inclination to engage in newsworthy community activities. As a result, much of my research centered on finding true and credible accounts that could be reasonably implied about their lives.

This is as much the story of the early settlers of the Town of Ashford, in northern Cattaraugus County, New York, as it is about a particular family. From the *Pioneer History of the Holland Purchase of Western New York*, by O. Turner (1849), I learned about the terrain and the unfettered arrival of the white man to the previously forbidden territory of the Seneca Nation, "Keepers of the Western Door". From *History of Cattaraugus County*, edited by Franklin Ellis (1879), *History of the Original Town of Concord*, by Erasmus Briggs (1883), and *Historical Gazetteer and Biographical Memoir of Cattaraugus County*, edited by William Adams (1893), I learned of the people who came to this region and the nature of the land. *UPSTATE TRAVELS, British Views of*

*Nineteenth Century New York,* edited by Roger Hayden (1982) confirmed the rugged nature of the land and the reason it took so long for settlers to venture across the Cattaraugus Creek. *The History of Cheesemaking in New York State,* by Eunice R. Stamm (1991) shed light on one of the area's significant 19th century industries.

The World Wide Web led me to Ancestry.com for family life facts, and to CrookedLakeReview.com and PaintedHills.org where I found fascinating pioneer adventures that seemed applicable to my story's family.

I deeply appreciate the time extended by Bill King (Town of Ashford Historian) and Dave Batterson (Town of Concord Historian). Their input was instrumental in preparing a historically accurate tale. Joline Hawkins took a genuine interest and supplied me with much reference material at the Lucy Bentley Center, home of the Concord Historical Society. *[Dear Miss Bentley. I remember her well from evenings spent at the Springville Library in my youth.]* Conversations with Barbara Crandell, Norm Pabst, Ron Klahn and Joel Maul provided further insight.

I cannot thank Pat Iacuzzi, a friend and retired art teacher, enough for her offer of time and talent. From my meager selection of old snapshots, and the images I envisioned as I wrote the story, Pat drew two excellent portrayals of the house as it is believed to have existed in the 1850's.

One can never accomplish a successful outcome without many friends who are willing to participate month after month as first drafts become properly edited material.

Many thanks to Kim Gore and the Greece Barnes & Noble Writer's Group and to the Lilac City Rochester Writers (LCRW). These two groups have offered wonderful chapter by chapter feedback. Finally, to those who stood by me – to my wife, Jackie, who kept my grammar and punctuation readable and endured multiple re-reads; to Linda Murray who never fails to encourage me; to writer friends: Steve Yates, Pat Gore, Pat Kennedy and Giovanna May; to several who, after reviewing the completed first draft, offered excellent advice: Jessica Pegis, Brian and Marge Oyer, Pat Iacuzzi and Sue Iekel-Johnson.

To all who helped this book come about, my heartfelt thanks!

# Alone

The old house stood silent and sad along a lonely stretch of country road not far from the busy state highway. Not many people passed by anymore. Everyone seemed to be rushing here and there on their way to someplace else.

It wasn't like that before. Before, the paved two lane road out in front had been the main route of travel between Springville and Ellicottville. The house remembered when Edies Road used to be called the Ashford Hollow Road and, before that, the Franktown Road. But, that was a long time ago. Nobody thought about that now. In fact, few even knew what it was like before the big highway was built.

The house sat on his stone foundation and leaned on his hand-hewn beams, thinking about the past while the cold April rain splattered on his roof. He felt terribly lonely and memories of the passing years flooded to the surface. He missed the old times; missed the people who had lived within his protective walls for so many years.

1

The house smiled (if a house can smile) as he recalled a little boy who lived here when they first built Route 219. The boy must have been about ten or eleven years old. He was terribly excited that summer. *When was that? Oh, I know, 1955.* Dump trucks rumbled by, hauling dirt and stones to and from the highway construction that crawled across the land just the other side of the ravine. The boy would watch and wave every chance he got. Then, one day, he had a brilliant idea. He ran to the kitchen, found a supply of paper cups, mixed some ice cold lemonade and set up a roadside stand to earn extra money. Trucks soon lined the narrow asphalt surface in front of his house, the big red rigs grumbling as they waited, while drivers purchased and drained tall glasses of lemonade. *Ah, the memories.*

As one thought led to another, the house grew more depressed by the minute. Scoby Road was gone now, gobbled up by the new State highway. U.S. Rt. 219 entered the Town of Ashford over a long bridge high at the crest of the cliffs that edged the Cattaraugus Creek. Even that bridge was gone now, replaced by a newer, bigger, higher four-lane bridge. From that point it followed Scoby's path to a nearby spot, wiping out the old dirt road forever.

The house searched back, all the way back to his beginning in 1854. Good old Scoby Road had always been there. It carried the name of one of the Town's early settlers.

Alexander Scoby had migrated to Western New York with his family at the age of seventeen. In 1827 he and his new bride found property along the Cattaraugus Creek at a place called "Transit Falls". There, he built a saw mill and a grist mill. For the next forty years he operated "Scoby Mills" with his wife and their nine children, supplying nearby families with the planks that built their buildings and flour that rendered delicious meals prepared by devoted housewives. When, in 1862, Scoby built a bridge across the creek, the road leading to his mill became one of the few points of access across the sometimes wild flow of water that separated Cattaraugus County from Erie County, its neighbor to the north.

Of course, the house wasn't around when Scoby built his mill, but he knew his facts. He had heard the boys in that first family, the family that built him, talk about the saw mill before going to sleep in the loft one night. They had spent most of the day there while old man Scoby milled their logs and returned with a supply of boards that would be used to build a new shed.

That's how the house got most of his information. Every evening, when the sun went down and the fire in the hearth settled into a few glowing embers, the family headed for bed. Before the soft and even breathing of the girls and the orchestra of snores from the boys, there was sure to be talk. He tried to listen carefully, soaking up the fascinating details of the day's activities. He had learned his history well. This was the story of the pioneers who settled in the Town of Ashford along the northern border of Cattaraugus County.

Only three decades before the house itself was built, the land that was to become the Town of Ashford, was a dense primal forest inhabited only by deer, bear, cougars and their smaller wildlife companions. Nearly uninhabitable, it was, nevertheless, the hunting grounds for the Native American population who had lived in Western New York since the ice of the second glacial period receded to the north ten thousand years ago. When, in 1794, the Seneca Nation agreed to settle on several limited reservations, the Holland Land Company surveyed and parceled off sizeable lots for sale, and the area became available for settlers.

Farmers from the more populated areas of Central New York and from New England read the Land Company's promotional material and took interest. Soon settlers began to relocate to take advantage of this fertile virgin soil. Though he was, by no means, among the first to be built by these pioneers, House knew of the dreams these settlers dreamed. He had been created by the hands of a man whose family had developed their land into a successful farm in the mid-1800's.

The world was different now. Today, no one could make a decent living by operating a small farm like in the past. House missed that. Now, vacant and cold, he sat as he had been sitting for 160 years. How he wished he could again offer shelter to some nice family.

The sound of a car and voices interrupted his reminiscing. By the side of the road not far away, two

4

young women were standing next to a car while a soaking rain poured down from the grey sky above.

*     *     *

Jessie and her friend had been out all day scouting the area as they explored Rose Mary's Native American heritage. Now they were stuck with a dead car on some backwoods road in the sticks of Western New York. Not only that. Jessie had forgotten to recharge her cell phone the night before and it was dead as a doornail. The cold April rain pelted them as they surveyed the useless car. She gave one tire a sharp kick and yelped at the unexpected pain.

Rose Mary just smiled and shook her head.

"Come on, Jess. There's no sense in hurting yourself over a broken down car. What if we duck into that abandoned house over there?"

She swung her head around in the direction of a shabby old house one hundred feet away and beads of rain spun off her straight black hair. "At least we'll be able to move around instead of sitting out the storm in your VW."

Jessie looked where her friend was pointing. The empty weather-beaten farmhouse was in desperate shape and in need of repair. Here and there loose shingles hung on an angle by one nail. Fresh paint would only be a beginning. Below the shingles, the stone foundation was coming undone. It looked like no one had lived there for at least a few years. Her eyes turned back to her friend. With a bitter smile she sighed,

"Sure, why not."

Gathering up what they could easily carry, the two raced toward the house under cover of jackets more suited to hold out the cold than the rain. As Rosie reached for the doorknob, the door seemed to open by itself. The two soggy twenty-somethings looked at each other, shrugged their shoulders and stepped inside.

"Well, that's a start." Jessie commented. "At least we'll be dry."

She surveyed the well-worn trappings of a tired old kitchen neglected by years of use without upkeep. The spot where a refrigerator had once stood was empty and a gas stove sat against one wall. A metal table with a yellow Formica top and a matching bottom shelf stood on rollers and was accompanied by two padded but badly ripped kitchen chairs. The counter top looked like it had been built in the 1950's. It formed a cover over several beat-up wooden cabinets, one of which sported an active mouse hole. As she walked past the sink, Jessie idly tried the faucet. A tiny stream of cloudy water gurgled out. Making a face, she jammed the handle back to the off position and kept on moving.

Meanwhile, Rose Mary struck off on her own to tour the rest of the house. She passed through what must have once been a dining room. The home's bathroom stood off to her right. Looking down at the floor before moving on, she spotted a large metal grate that offered evidence of a once useful furnace. It had probably provided central heat for the entire house. She bit her lip and hesitated a moment before stepping on it to enter the next room. Safely across, she looked up and let out a whoop that brought Jessie to her side.

"What's going on, Rosie? Are you all right?"

By this time Rose Mary was kneeling in front of a wood burning stove. She turned to respond. "Oh, I'm sorry. I didn't mean to frighten you. It's just that I found this stove and it looks useable." A pile of dry wood was sitting next to the contraption. "Maybe we can get a fire going, and warm up a bit."

As Jessie came up behind her friend, Rosie began loading a few sticks of kindling and wads of paper into the black potbellied stove held up by three legs and a chunk of 4x4 wood laying on its side. A box of matches advertising The Leland House lay on the chunk of wood. Jessie picked up the matches to examine them.

"There's only three in here, Rosie. Good luck," and she handed it over to her friend.

"No sweat, Jess. I'm Seneca. I can light a fire. Besides, I have a good feeling about this. The spirit of the past is all over this place."

At that, she struck the first match. The micro burst of instant light extinguished itself as quickly as it started. Rosie lit the second match. Shielding the flame, she guided it toward the crumpled up paper. A tiny fire popped up and began to spread, then suddenly withered into a red glow and died away. A worried look overshadowed her usually bright brown eyes as she looked up and saw Jessie's smirk.

Stepping back just a bit, Jessie held up her hands as if to ward off any blame. "Better you than me, Rosie. You're the one in charge of fire."

Rosie was determined to succeed. She hovered over the last match as she pulled it out of the box. Just before striking it, Jessie heard her mutter, more to herself than to anyone else, ". . . gonna need a little help here!"

A brisk blaze again took hold of the wadded tuft of paper. Only, this time, a faint breath of air seemed to come out of nowhere, fanning the flame. The two watched as the inside of the stove began to brighten and a corner of the wood kindling began to burn.

"You did it, Rosie. Good job."

Rose Mary, though, appeared more amazed than triumphant when she looked up.

"Did you feel that? Did you feel that little rush of air? Where did it come from? That's what did it. That's what lit the fire. The timing couldn't have been more perfect."

The wood crackled as warm air began to flow around the two stranded women. Jessie and Rose Mary, ready to accept any small comfort by this time, rubbed their hands over the heat. As they stood there together, a sound sort of like a gentle sigh, seemed to come out of nowhere. Both looked up, mentally weighing what they had heard. Then, looking at each other, they spoke almost in unison,

"Was that you? – No!"

Though each looked over her shoulder to see if someone had entered the room, neither wanted to leave the warm air now flowing from the potbellied stove. They were glad to have a fire to counteract the effects of April's cold rain and drew their full attention back to the iron relic that was now spreading its wealth around the room.

Again, a gentle sigh seemed to escape from the walls that surrounded them.

# Looking Back

As the rain continued outdoors, the room inside grew more comfortable. Jessie and Rosie realized they would be stuck here for a while. Making the best of it, they joked and kidded with each other to ease the situation. But, eventually, that grew thin and silence ruled. Finally, Jessie thought of a good way to fill the void.

"So, Rosie, tell me about your ancestors."

Rose Mary turned, cocked her head to one side, and gazed at her friend. She had a faraway look in her eyes, almost like her mind was reaching back, way back, to a time before the white man.

"My great-great-great grandmother was the Clan Mother of the Bear Clan about the time the Seneca moved into this area."

"That sounds like a big deal," Jessie quipped. "But, weren't the men in charge? What did a Clan Mother do?"

Rosie's smile faded and she let out a long sigh.

"Are you kidding? The Seneca Nation was a matriarchal society. The Clan Mother was the Clan's real leader. The boys might have gone off to play and hunt, and, typical of men everywhere, gone away to fight wars. But, the oldest woman in the Clan, the Clan Mother, was the one who had the final say about anything important. She was the one who chose the Chief and she had the power to unseat him if he wasn't acting in the best interest of the Clan."

"Really? That's awesome."

A whisper of air circulated around the room and the walls almost seemed to hum. The girls looked at each other, then cautiously looked over their shoulders. Though neither felt particularly threatened, both sensed a presence. They said nothing.

"So-o-o," Jessie again questioned. "What's a clan?"

"Oh! Well, the Seneca Nation was, and still is, divided into six clans. They are family lines. You've heard of the longhouses, haven't you?"

"Yea."

"Well, a typical village might have several longhouses and each one belonged to a particular clan."

"So the whole extended family all lived in one house?" Jessie questioned. "My grandparents moved in with us for a year before Grandpa died." She looked down at her hands, then shoved them out of sight in her pockets. "You can't believe the chaos in our house because of it."

"Well," Rosie responded, "from what I've learned, the long houses were about twenty feet wide and could be up to two hundred feet long depending upon how many families lived there. Everybody had a section on one side or the other, and shared a fire pit with the family across from them." Rosie leaned back to check on her own fire. "The sections were made up of two-tiered bunks. The family slept on the bottom bunks and stored their goods on the top bunks. It seems, though, they really didn't spend much time in the long house beyond sleeping."

Jessie summed up the long house discussion. "I don't care how big a house is, with the whole extended family in one longhouse, I can't imagine what it must have been like."

The crackling of wood in the stove had grown silent and Rosie realized it needed more fuel. Stretching, she pulled herself off the floor just enough to reach the stack of fire wood. Like she had done this all her life, she clicked open the door and tossed in two pieces. Then, just as quickly, pulled her head back as a burst of heat rushed out. Appearing deep in thought, she closed the latch and looked back at her friend.

"Frankly, Jessie, I'm intrigued by the whole story of how the Seneca got here in the first place."

Jessie looked puzzled. "Weren't they always here? They're the 'Keepers of the Western Door' aren't they?"

"Yes, they are. But, until the mid-1600's, they were pretty much isolated to the Genesee Valley south of Rochester. About that time they went to war with the Erie Nation who lived along the south shore of Lake Erie." She screwed up her face. "Nobody's really sure why. Basically, they exterminated the Erie. The Seneca were fierce fighters, and everyone, both the white man and the other tribes, pretty much kept clear of their territory until the Revolutionary War.

"After the War, General Sullivan swept through the Genesee Valley and annihilated every single Seneca village. Our leaders realized they would never be able to stop the white man. So, rather than move to the far west, like a lot of other nations were doing, they decided to give up their right to most of this territory. In exchange, they demanded a guarantee that the White Man's government provide them with several small but exclusive reservations. That way, some thought, they could carry on peacefully with the new settlers. They all knew that eventually the settlers would come whether they liked it or not. It was a pretty sore topic within the Nation for quite a while.

"For a long time after our people moved onto the reservations and before the settlers actually arrived we continued to hunt on this land.

"But, when they did live here, where did they live? How did they live?" Jessie was a reporter and, like many others, maintained an ongoing fascination with stories about the Native American population. This could be a prize winning story.

"Good question, Jess. As far as I could find out, there are no identified villages in this particular area. But, the hunting parties came here, sometimes for quite a while. It's likely they set up temporary camps along the streams. There's evidence of those sites on the banks of the

Cattaraugus and Connoisarauley Creeks. One fellow I was talking to recently said that, when he was a boy, he used to go down to 'The Breakers' every spring. He could always find arrow heads along the banks of the stream near the bridge."

"Cool!"

"The creeks would have been a means of easy travel for them and, since fish was a staple in their diet, also a great source of food while they were in the area."

The two were silent for a moment as Rosie stared off somewhere into the past. Suddenly her face lit up and she started again.

"I'll bet you didn't know the Seneca women were really the first farmers."

"No, I didn't."

"While the men were out hunting and fishing, the women and children planted and tended large gardens. They grew what they called 'The Three Sisters'."

"Three sisters!" Jessie screwed up her face. "What, on earth, were the 'Three Sisters'?"

Rose Mary laughed. "That got me, too when I heard it. . . . corn, beans and squash. The three were planted together in a mound. They were considered gifts from the Great Spirit. The corn stalk was a natural pole for the bean vine to climb, and the bean plant helped fertilize the soil. The squash plant acted like mulch and kept the soil moist. It was a stringy plant, so it also kept the animals away while all three plants were growing."

Jessie leaned back and smiled. "Cool."

14

# A Voice

The house was content. As the two girls carried on their conversation, he hummed to himself. The warmth of the fire creeping into his walls and floor felt wonderful. His old joints, too, welcomed the warm breath of the burning wood. This harmless invasion was a rare treat after the previous cold and lonely winter. By the season's end, mounds of snow had practically hidden the house from what little traffic passed by.

It almost made one want to join in. But, the house knew from experience he would frighten these girls half to death if he said anything. *We houses are alive, you know,* House thought to himself. *We have a spirit. We shelter and protect the families who depend on us. You just have to be willing to listen.* Somehow he knew Rosie could feel him – might even be able to hear him if he said something. He had seen the look on her face at the front door, and, surely she had recognized how he helped her light the fire. Rosie was tuned in, her spirit somehow connected to the surrounding environment.

*This Jessie, though.* House wasn't quite sure how she would react if he spoke right now. He could tell Jessie was a non-believer. She looked like someone who would demand proof; one of those rational people who would end up shaking her head and walking away.

House could accept the fact that a person might leave screaming. Fear was a logical response and he had seen it happen before. Jessie, on the other hand, seemed like one of those obstinate people who could only see the world as black or white, living or dead, breathing or inanimate. Those were the ones to be reckoned with. Was Jessie one of them? House wasn't quite sure.

Rose Mary was different than Jessie. She would believe; she would be in his corner. Maybe Rose Mary could convince Jessie to stick around long enough to listen.

House searched his memory, all the way back to his youth, to a time when he had just been built. *There must be something I've heard about the Seneca when they lived here. Something I can tell them that would pique their interest enough to really talk to me.*

**"Oh, yea!"**

House was so caught up in his thoughts, he didn't even realize he had just spoken aloud. But, from the way the two visitors jerked their heads back, the way Rosie's eyes darted about the room, the way Jessie grabbed Rosie's arm, he knew they had heard him.

"What was that?" Jessie was on her feet and searching, looking about the room for some kind of life. She looked over at Rose Mary, bewildered.

"Did you hear that?"

Rosie nodded but appeared to have lost her voice. The look on her face though, told Jessie that she, too, was alarmed.

"Who's there?" Jessie tried to sound firm.

Only silence reigned, as House thought it best to remain quiet. Now, both were on their feet and demanding an answer. Rosie took her turn.

"We know someone's here. Whoever you are, come out."

House realized he would have to say something. Somehow, he had to calm them. But, he knew – he just knew – the next words he spoke would do exactly the opposite. Finally, fearing what they might do next, House spoke again.

"Please don't be afraid. I didn't mean to alarm you." He watched as each of them, eyes wide with apprehension, slowly turned her head, searching – searching. But, no one was there.

"I've been listening to your story, Rose Mary. I love stories. I got carried away and spoke out loud."

"What? Who are you? Why don't you show yourself?"

House focused his full attention on Rose Mary. Maybe, just maybe, he could convince her he was real. Jessie, on the other hand, was staring, her mouth wide

17

open. There would be no sense trying to speak directly to her. He would have to rely on Rosie, the descendent of a Seneca, to convince Jessie they weren't both crazy.

House sighed, a sound both recognized right away. "People say that walls have ears. What no one seems to realize is that we also have a voice."

At this point Jessie was on her feet and moving toward the kitchen door. It didn't matter to her that it was still raining outside. Her lips were trembling and a cold chill crawled across every surface of her body. "Rain or no rain," she announced, "this is crazy. Let's get out of here."

"Please don't go."

Sadness marked his voice as House pleaded, "Rose Mary, you noticed when I opened the front door. You sensed my presence when I helped you light the fire. I know that, right now, you're beginning to understand. Your Seneca blood is telling you you're not crazy. Please help Jessie understand you're safe."

After a l-o-n-g minute Rose Mary finally spoke.

"Hang on, Jess. I know what's happening is downright crazy. But, my ancestors were one with the earth and all the animals and creatures of the earth. I once heard of a Chief Seattle who said, *'This we know - the Earth does not belong to man - man belongs to the Earth. All things are connected like the blood which unites one family. All things are connected.'* I can't explain why, but I'm not uncomfortable with this. Not yet, anyway. Can't we just sit tight and see what happens?"

Jessie just stared at her friend. Her shoulders dropped just a bit as she responded, "Yea – well, okay. But this whole thing gives me the creeps."

As the two women sat down, House let out another sigh. It sounded and felt like the wind whistling down the chimney.

At least partially accepted for the moment, the old house began to share.

"I wasn't around when this area was occupied by the Seneca Nation. But, I heard the first family who lived here talk about something that might interest you."

"So, let's have it." Jessie leaned back against the wall and crossed her arms in total defiance. House wisely chose to ignore her and continued.

"There's this rock. It's a real sight to see – bigger than anything you'll ever see around here. It must have been a landmark for the Seneca who hunted in this area. It's as big as the body of a dump truck; probably eight feet high and ten feet across. It's got to be at least twenty feet long. Every boy who ever  lived here climbed on it when they were up in the woods. One of the dads thought it was probably dragged here from somewhere else during the last ice age 10,000 years ago."

Jessie, still incredulous at their situation, spoke up. "Yea. So what? What would that have to do with the Seneca people?"

"It had to have been a draw for them, Jessie. As Rose Mary said, the Native American population was extremely close to nature. They lived with it; understood it. Their lives were intertwined with the animals and the very earth itself. A boulder that big and that unusual must have drawn their interest."

"So, that's all you have to offer?" Jessie almost sneered.

"Jessie!" Rose Mary, hands on her hips, glared at her friend in utter amazement. "Really?"

House understood Jessie's reaction, though. This situation had really thrown her. She was obviously a smart, savvy woman, but she just wasn't ready to engage in a conversation with an inanimate object.

"It's all right, Rosie. I understand. It will take Jessie some time to warm up to me."

"Hello! I'm right here."

Jessie stood straight as a rod, her jaw set, her tight muscles ready to snap. Against every grain of sanity she was, in fact, engaging in a conversation with a house. A HOUSE, damn it!

Rosie saw that her friend was unsettled – tense – agitated. She'd never seen her friend like this before, but she wanted to get down to business and learn what she could learn. At the moment the only thing she could do was to ignore Jessie's protest.

"Tell me, Mr. House, how long have you been around?"

"Well, Michael and Sarah, the people who built me, first came to this area in 1848. They had a little piece of property several miles away. Then, in 1853, Michael bought this property and built me."

"Tell us more. We're all ears."

"Hm-m-m." House hummed for a moment. "Let me see, where do I begin?"

\*          \*          \*

The long ride on the Erie Canal from Herkimer to Black Rock was finally over. Michael and Sarah had heard stories about the canal, how many of the people who earned their living from this waterway were loud and coarse. For them, though, it had been a quiet trip and rather pleasurable.

Leaving the line boat, they gathered the children, hitched the oxen to their wagon, and began the more difficult journey over land. They had been cautioned to travel during the late summer months. The roads would be drier, the creeks easier to cross and the weather more comfortable for the women and children.

Michael was delighted to find that the road to Springville, the last viable community on the way to their destination, was a plank road. Such surfaces were few and far between. It looked, to Michael, like a primitive musical keyboard as it stretched out to the crest of the next horizon.

Pleased at the prospect of easier than expected travel, he told the family they should arrive at their destination within a couple of days.

It was the end of the first day's travel. Cresting the first of many hills on their way, the family gazed in awe at the panoramic display that lay before them. Row upon row of hills, each slightly more elevated than the last, stretched out in the distance. Except for the path they were following, they saw nothing but forest. Somewhere out there, in the midst of all those trees was their cousin's home. A small log cabin, built and abandoned by some earlier settler, awaited their use until they could purchase land and build a house of their own on a parcel big enough for a productive farm.

The view, in some ways, terrified Sarah. As she looked out at this magnificent natural beauty, she was torn by conflicting emotions. She suddenly realized just how much her life was about to change. She could never forget the warmth of her family's homestead near the banks of the Mohawk River. That was home, and *home* meant family, safety, comfort. Yet, soon this wooded patch of landscape that had not long ago been the forbidden territory of the Seneca Nation would be their home. While her heart pined for the comforts offered back along the Mohawk, her head knew the very idea of fertile soil, yet to be cultivated, gave new hope for Michael and their young family.

Herkimer had been a wonderful place to grow up and start a family, but that part of the state was getting crowded and available land in that area was at a premium. The time had come to find a new home, to begin new family traditions. It was their turn to encounter this new territory that was being talked about so much. This would become *home* soon enough.

A blue haze mixed with the light of the setting sun and made the hills look almost mystical. Standing with Sarah and the children at his side, Michael fixed his eyes on the land in front of him, searching. Then, lifting his arm and pointing in the direction of one particular range of hills, he called to his children.

"There she be, Children. Soon enough we be clearin' a patch of forest fer our new home." He looked down at the heads of his tired bunch and smiled. "But, right now, we all needs ta be gettin' some rest fer tomorrow's trip. After yer Ma fix some vittles fer supper, we will set up ta sleep here till the mornin'."

23

The next day, as the family started up, two oxen pulled the heavy farm wagon laden with all the family's possessions. A solitary cow, hitched to the rear of the cart, lowed mournfully. Too young to walk, six-year-old George and five-year-old Conrad rode on the wagon and kept an eye on their younger sister. Two-year-old Lavina, though, just hung on tight, too afraid of falling to move about. Seven-year-old Simon walked with his father while the three oldest, Mary, Catherine and Nancy, kept up a gleeful pace with their mother, excited by the prospect of this new place to live.

For the children, this was a great adventure. For mother and father, it offered the hope of a secure future for their growing family. Michael knew about farming, and this new land would, he felt, eventually reward him for his hard work.

*　　　*　　　*

As House paused in his story, Jessie let out a sigh, stood up, and stepped to the window. A hard, searching look crossed her face as she stared out at the drizzle that continued to fall.

"I just can't grasp how difficult it must have been for Sarah. After all, they must have left a reasonably comfortable home. The Mohawk Valley has been populated since the late 17$^{th}$ century." She took a long look around the room. "I mean, how does one decide what to bring and what to leave behind?"

24

"I dunno, Jess." Rose Mary, already mesmerized by the tale, almost whispered as she spoke. "I think it would be pretty exciting. Imagine the whole idea of starting fresh, of claiming a piece of land and turning it into a productive farm." She paused, then added, "Sure, it would be difficult, but what a sense of accomplishment."

House just kept still and listened. He relished the conversations that took place under his roof. He'd heard them all. The secrets whispered in darkened bedrooms, the stories of life in these hills, the jockeying for position in the family, even the outright battles that usually ended with a slammed door and the muffled sound of sobbing from the one left behind.

He cherished these moments, all of them. Sometimes he would have to stifle a laugh at the antics of the people who lived here. Sometimes his timbers would sag in sympathy, his windows searching the heavens for a little ray of light to replace the sadness. As a house, it was his job to shelter and protect his charges. When the threat was from the outside, well, that was easy. But, when the family itself was in conflict, House found his responsibility downright heartbreaking.

Suddenly Jessie turned back from the window. Though she didn't quite know where to look, she addressed the house with a sense of purpose. An interesting story was unfolding and the journalist in her finally needed to hear it.

"When did you say Michael and Sarah made this trip?"

"It was, ah-h, in 1848," House replied.

As a reporter, Jessie made it her business to know the local history. "That had to be at least twenty-five or thirty years after the first pioneers arrived. Wasn't the Town incorporated in 1824?"

"Well, yes," House responded. "In this general area, the Cattaraugus Creek and the steep hills and cliffs at the creek's edge were serious barriers for a very long time. I've heard the first settlers crossed the creek about 1819 and, when they did, they faced a wall of trees not easy to penetrate. For the first ten years after that, you could count the total number of people living around here on your fingers."

House thought for a moment, then continued. "One time a neighbor brought a newspaper article here about some fellow from Great Britain who had written about his trek from Springville to Ellicottville in 1816. It read:

"My journey the next day, from Springville to the Cattaraugus land office, (18 miles) was through an unbroken desert for 16 miles. It was the most fatiguing journey I ever experienced, and one that I almost despaired of ever accomplishing, - having no track, but marks on trees. . . " *(From Emmanuel Howitt, "Selections from Letters Written During a Tour through the United States, in the Summer and Autumn of 1819 . . . Nottingham J. Dunn, 1820)*

Rosie broke into a gleeful smile and cocked her head. "The guy sounds pretty overwhelmed. I wonder what his reaction would have been if he had run into a Seneca hunting party." She laughed and added, "But, tell us about Michael and Sarah's arrival here."

# The Breakers

House resumed his tale.

\*         \*         \*

On a sunny October afternoon in 1853, Michael stood high on the hill. It had been five years since he and his family had arrived at this wild frontier. Finally he had a piece of property he could turn into a productive farm. It had been a difficult beginning, the cramped quarters offered by his cousin, the small piece of property he had initially purchased to sustain his growing family.

Now he owned a piece of rolling, wooded land where he could build his own home, till the fertile soil and tend to his growing herd of cattle. From this clearing, he could see nearly the entire 54 acres he had purchased. As his eyes swept down and across the tree filled slope at his feet, he took a good look at all the tall trees and pondered,

*Plenty o' good lumber here. Now, where ta build the house?*

Part way down the hill the slope leveled off a little before dropping into a deep gully where a stream gurgled its way to the Connoisarauley Creek. Again distracted, *Good. Fresh drinkin' water fer the cattle.*

Michael's eyes followed the rising slope on the other side of the valley to a patch of green tree-filled land that crested and disappeared over the next rise. He knew the west boundary of his property ended along the edge of old man Scoby's road. It was out of sight from where he stood, but he could see it in his mind's eye.

"T'was a good deal. We can make a livin' offa this land"

At $2.00 an acre, the agent, Nicholas Devereaux, was making a handsome profit, but it was a reasonable price and Michael held no grudge. He shook his head as he thought about Devereaux and what he had accomplished. A land agent, he had purchased 418,000 acres of deep almost uninhabitable hilly forest from the Holland Land Company a few years ago. The land extended south from the Cattaraugus Creek to the Pennsylvania border.

In one conversation Nick had told Michael, "I knew I was taking a risk. Under this mass of jungle-like timber, though, the land is rich and tillable." What he now had to offer was a drawing card for many farmers willing to relocate from the more eastern areas of New York State and from New England.

29

Nick had referred to the area as "Franktown". *Franktown!* Michael's thoughts buzzed back to their recent conversation. Devereaux had said, "The Springville Post Office services this area twice a week. So many Franks live around here they have labeled it 'Franktown' after Henry Frank and his two sons, Andrew and Jacob. They were the first to arrive in 1819. Their offspring are scattered across the area." Michael knew several already. Fred and Nancy, Lawrence and Lydia. They were practically his next door neighbors.

This land was a good place to settle, close enough to Springville that Michael could buy his supplies and sell off his surplus produce once in a while. *If only it wasn't for those breakers,* Michael thought. *They are something to be reckoned with even in the best of conditions.* He shuttered as he remembered that first encounter with the steep hills on their original trip five years ago.

*       *       *

That day, the road leading out of Springville to Franktown was a dusty surface, far less traveled than the one on the way into town. Michael had been warned about the Breakers, a narrow valley surrounded by steep hills and cliffs. The area could be completely impassible during springtime floods and nearly impossible to navigate in winter. Fortunately, it was now summer. The road would be dry and the creek contained within its banks.

Michael stood at the top of a steep incline leading into the Breakers. He saw signs of earlier mud slides. In some places the road tipped dangerously to one side. Deciding to walk its entire length before venturing down with the wagon, he looked back and called out, "I be lookin' at this here hill fer a time. Be good ta feed the little ones, Sarah." Then, to the older boys, "Git some water fer the animals." ...and he disappeared over the crest.

On his return, Michael gathered the family and prepared for the descent into the valley. While the trip down was uneventful, going up the other hill

(*From "History of Cattaraugus County, New York" 1879, by Franklin Ellis*)

after crossing the bridge was another story.

The creek itself seemed harmless enough. It arrived, bubbling past a wide green field where, no doubt, the recently departed Seneca had surely made their hunting camps. Passing under a covered bridge on a stony bed of shale, it made a gentle turn before disappearing between steep cliffs on both sides.

Hooves echoed with each step as their wagon crossed within the wooden supports of the covered bridge.

31

Michael led, his hand sitting lightly on the broad neck of one ox. He knew his animals well, and, at the moment, he sensed they were both a bit skittish.

For the boys this was a nice change from the humdrum of earlier well-traveled trails. They looked here and there, scampering down to the creek's edge and wading across, basking in the coolness of the water. Then, climbing back up the embankment on the other side, they hooted and hollered to express their excitement.

"Silence."

Michael's stern voice brought their activities to a sudden halt.

"The Ladies (He always referred to Missie and Millie, his two oxen, as 'the Ladies') be nervous enough without you boys runnin' around like a pack of wild animals."

The steep hill before them dropped off dangerously close to the road's edge, falling away to the stream below. Except for Michael, the entire family stayed a short distance behind the cart.

At the halfway point, the road turned away from the stream. Michael could see the crest and was about to let out a sigh of relief. Suddenly Missie stumbled on a loose rock and went down hard on her knees. Millie lurched away from her partner, dragging the injured Missie. An agonizing bellow cut through the air, followed by a loud CRACK as Missie's leg snapped in two. The family watched in horror as the tethered pair of oxen reacted, each in their own way.

"Lord have mercy. We gonna lose the load." Michael muttered to himself. Then, to the others. "Hear now. Block those wheels. We about to lose everything."

Sarah had been watching her husband. Now she turned to search the sides of the road. Surely there must be some rock or chunk of wood. George pulled out his newly acquired pocket knife and cut through a rope holding down some of their furnishings.

"Conrad, catch this."

He tossed a wooden footstool down to his brother who grabbed it and jammed it behind one wheel. Meanwhile, Sarah was dragging a broken tree limb she had spotted to block the other rear wheel.

Down on her side, Missie continued to bawl in pain as Michael quickly loosened the yoke to free her. Unless he could separate the two oxen, he was sure the wagon and all their possessions would be lost over the edge of the road.

"George – Simon, get up here. See if you can keep Millie quiet. Back'r off. We gotta get the wagon around Missie."

The two oldest scrambled to heed their father.

"Easy, now, Millie. Easy."

Simon was best friends with Millie. She would listen to him. Simon just knew it.

"Easy, Millie. Now haw, Millie – haw. He touched her left flank and she followed.

As Simon guided the wagon around their injured ox, Michael looked up.

"Sarah, take the little ones and follow Simon to the top of the hill. Then wait there." Then, to George, "George, get my gun 'n some ammunition."

"No, Papa – No" Lavina cried. "You can't shoot Missie."

Sarah, tears welling up in her eyes, grabbed the girl's shoulder. Twisting her around, she ordered, "March, young woman. You'll not be talkin' back to your father."

Then, gathering the girls, she led the family to the top of the hill. There, next to the loaded wagon and one ox, the family waited in silence.

The sudden crack of a gunshot startled everyone and made them jump. It echoed through the valley and up to the rim where they waited. Then came another.

Mary, Catherine and Nancy buried their heads in Sarah's long full dress. The boys were off somewhere, each unseen. Sarah wiped fresh tears from her face but said nothing.

An hour passed. Finally, Michael appeared, his head down, hunched over like an old man. Stripped of his shirt, he carried a heavy package over one shoulder. His voice cracked as he looked at his wife and children.

"Best we stop here for the night. We lost a lotta time on that there hill." No one spoke in response.

\*     \*     \*

House paused in his story. "Poor Michael. He didn't tell that story often, but when he did . . .well, I could feel the pain he felt that day. Sometimes he acted hard and tough in front of his children, but inside he was just a softy. When he lost that ox, sure, he lost a valuable working animal. But it was more than that. These animals were his companions. Caring for them was more than a responsibility. It was personal."

\*       \*       \*

Back on the hillside, Michael looked up at the greyish clouds that were scattered across the October sky and shook away the distressing memories of that day five years ago. His wandering mind returned to the reality of today's decision. With nine children to shelter, building a proper house was his first and most important priority. His daughters were coming of age. Simon was thirteen years old, George and Conrad not far behind. A baby was on the way. He drew his attention back to the scene in front of him and began to focus on the narrow piece of property in front of the gully. The Franktown Road passed next to that stretch. The land seemed, he thought, just level enough to allow room for a house – a barn – maybe a few smaller buildings.

Nodding his head to affirm his thoughts he whispered, "That be the spot."

Now satisfied, he withdrew from the clearing and trudged back down past massive maple and elm trees that covered the landscape. Soon most of them would be cut down and milled into the wide thick planks necessary for their new home's framework and walls. These trees that had, for decades, protected the woodland wildlife, would soon keep his family safe, dry and comfortable. The soft mat of leaf enriched undergrowth crunched under his boots as he plodded down the hill.

# Mama Bear

The wealth of hillside timber, tall straight trees that reached for the sun to feed on its rays, became the raw material for their new home. Working alongside his eldest three sons, Michael spent his days clearing the land. Tree by tree the foursome labored with saw and axe, to harvest useable tree trunks, leaving the stumps to rot away at their own pace or to be burned when time permitted. Stripped of their limbs and cut into transportable lengths, the subdued logs were carted to Scoby's mill on the banks of the Cattaraugus Creek. There, Scoby's able sons transformed them into the wide, thick planks needed to build their new home.

As they cleared the land of its trees, Michael prepared the rich soil and sowed the seeds for plants that would sustain his small retinue of service animals. Sarah and the girls, too, took advantage of the clearing nearest their future home. Even before the house was complete, they tilled the soil among the stumps and planted their

37

garden. Noting the success of the Seneca women from the nearby Cattaraugus Reservation, Sarah sowed "The Three Sisters", (corn, beans and squash). She was excited when she learned how the trio worked. The corn provided a natural pole for the bean vines, the beans added important nutrients to the soil, and the squash kept the soil moist and kept hungry animals away. In addition, when ripe, this combination would offer up plenty of food for the family table.

"Come along, Millie. We've got a lot of logs to deliver to old man Scoby today."

The ox lowed softly as she turned to look at the boy. The two had been working on this project for several days. She knew what she must do and trusted the sturdy teenager. Simon rolled out a long hemp rope to hook up to the next available log. Looping an end around the fallen tree trunk, he carefully draped the other over Millie's head and neck. Then, patting her hind quarter, he gave the order, "Get up, Millie." and guided her toward the waiting sleigh at the other end of the clearing.

Simon whistled to himself as they walked. He was happy his parents had found this patch of land. As soon as they finished building the house they would be moving from the tiny one room cabin near his cousin's place off Scoby Road. There was much to be done before that could happen, but he didn't mind. Life was good.

Lost in his thoughts, Simon never even saw the two bear cubs dart across his path. But, a moment later he heard their bark. At that, a larger than life mama bear arose from behind a patch of bramble bushes and, with her front paws spread wide, let out an angry roar.

Poor Millie took one look at the bear, her soft brown eyes now saucer-size and let out a snort. She turned and took off in the opposite direction. The log, some twenty feet behind her, suddenly became a whip aimed directly at Simon.

Simon knew of the wild animals that lived in this wooded paradise. Once he had actually seen a black bear and, from his bed in the middle of the night, had heard a cougar's nighttime cry. But, this was his first face-to-face encounter with anything larger than an angry raccoon. The mother bear's menacing roar was enough to raise the hair on your neck, and a cold chill ran down his back freezing him to the ground. For just an instant, he stood, looking at her, fully alert to the threat. But, in a flash, he realized a more imminent danger. The log, still tethered to Millie, was partially off the ground and about to rip off either his legs or his head, depending on its flight path when it hit him.

Ignoring the bears, Simon dove behind the stump of a tree that, only a few days ago, had been a part of the forest foliage. He landed face down in the muck of the winter's wetness and the saw dust and woodchips of previous work. As he landed, the wayward log hit the stump fully broadside and flew only inches over his now prone and mud painted body.

As Millie and the tethered log disappeared over the crest of a nearby hill, Simon lifted himself to his hands and knees. Shaking his head, he stood and began to check for cuts and bruises.

"Whew! That was a close one"

He began to brush himself off and turned to look at the condition of the stump. The bark where the log hit was torn away. A twelve-inch scar exposed a wide vertical crack where the log had broadsided the tree trunk. Simon stared in amazement as he faced it.

"Holy Mother of God. I could be dead now."

Suddenly he remembered the initial threat from the mother bear and looked up at the spot where she had appeared. But the thick patch of bushes was now quiet. Thankfully, the bears were nowhere to be seen. Millie's startled reaction and the out of control log had apparently been sufficient reason for mother and cubs to hightail it out of the area.

Several minutes later, Simon caught up with Millie. He draped his arm over her broad neck and rubbed his knuckles up and down the bridge of her nose.

"You okay, old girl? That was quite a scare."

The log was gone. The rope hung limp from Millie's neck, free of its burden. Millie's powerful legs had been too much for the length of hemp matter and it had snapped. Simon walked back along the path taken by the frightened ox and eventually located the log laying among a sea of tree stumps.

Meanwhile, Michael, George and Conrad were hauling stones from nearby Connoisarauley Creek unaware of Simon's struggle with the forces of nature. Along the rocky bed of this mountain stream there were ample places to find the thick, flat surfaces that, when properly joined, would form strong basement walls. The icy water left their hands and feet numb as they prodded and pounded at the sometimes submerged slabs of material. Oncoming winter, though, demanded that they hurry. Too soon the creeks would be buried under a skin of thick ice. The ravines, carved out of the Earth by rushing water over thousands of years, would be drifted over by deep snow banks.

As the day's activities came to a close and the family gathered for dinner, Simon shared his experience. His brothers wished they could have seen the bears. Sarah worried for his safety. The little ones ate, wide-eyed, while he told his story. Only Simon and Michael seemed to feel that it was just another day in the woods. But, when the gathering had disbursed and each was alone with his thoughts, both, in their own way, said a silent prayer of thanks to the God above who had spared Simon serious injury.

# A New Home

"Sarah loved her new home. ...I mean, what's not to like?" House interjected.

Rosie and Jessie could tell House was grinning, almost smirking. But, of course, they couldn't see it.

"Very funny." Jessie quipped. "Imagine, a house with a sense of humor."

By this time she had pulled out her pen and pad and was taking furious notes. The journalist in her recognized a good story. Waving her pen in the air, she went on. "There's what, six rooms down here and more space up at the top of the stairs? Even with teenage sons, how could Michael have built this?"

"Oh, Michael didn't build this place all at once," House replied. "It was actually built in three different stages. This room you're sitting in now was the core of the original house that Michael built. In the beginning, this was where they gathered for breakfast in the morning and where

Sarah made her magic. She was, by the way, a great cook. See that alcove at the end of the room? Originally that was the hearth."

Jessie turned and pointed to a 6x8 area partly enclosed by three walls. "You mean THAT? That was the hearth?"

"Yup."

House left it at that for a moment, letting the idea sink in as Jessie and Rosie focused on the spot. "Get the picture?"

"No. Well, yea. I guess – in a way. I mean, it's kind of hard to imagine that being a hearth, the way it looks now."

What the two women were looking at was a pretty little nook off the end of the living room. Each could envision a rocking chair with a side table and lamp. Maybe a couple of bookshelves hung on the opposite wall. The faint imprint of family portraits marked the back wall.

"In the 19th century," House continued, "the settlers had to build a sturdy hearth or they wouldn't survive. You've probably seen pictures of big city homes with their beautiful wood stoves and ornamental fireplaces. But, not out here – not where the settlers were just breaking ground. Pretty much, they couldn't transport such a large piece of equipment on an oxcart. They were lucky to bring the iron kettles and other basic cooking utensils they needed.

House hummed to himself for a moment and it felt, to the two women, like a warm breeze had come in to look around. Finally he continued. "Let me tell you what happened when it came time to move in."

*       *       *

Sarah was delighted when Michael announced they would be moving into the new house; that it was finally ready to live in. Her man had been spending way too much time away from their present home for the last month. Though only a few miles away, Michael and their second son, George, were already living there to finish the job. That way they saved the time otherwise lost by traveling back and forth every day.

It was a blustery January day. The winter sun played hide and seek with a scattering of low clouds that had discharged their offering on the previous day. As the wagon drew up to the front of the house, Sarah beheld a sturdy cottage.

The house sat back from the road thirty feet, or so, the land sloping down from where she stood. It was a might smaller than she would have liked, but it was new and inviting. Fresh cedar shingles peeked through the snow covered roof. A pair of windows accompanied the main entrance at the front. An overlarge extension on the left apparently housed the fireplace, as a stone chimney pointed upward from that area.

*( "Winter" With permission of Patricia Iacuzzi)*

Eight months pregnant, Sarah picked her way through the deep snow between the road and the house. She stopped for a moment with her hand on the door handle and looked back at Michael. With her eyes glued on her husband and a determined look on her face, she raised the latch to see her new home.

The main living area spread out in front of her and looked to be some thirty feet from front to back and just as wide. She spied a newly built rocking chair and a handsome side table next to a window at the back. The view from the window was a beautiful tree lined ravine at the rear of the house. Sarah also noted that her husband had built a large table and benches for meal time. These, she

45

realized, were offerings for a good beginning in their new home's living space.

An alcove, probably eight feet wide and six feet deep, a pioneer wife's dream kitchen, surrounded a large stone hearth. A scattering of cold ashes in the fireplace told her that her men had kept themselves warm and comfortable while they were away from her. A new iron cooking pot hung from a hook in the hearth and was accompanied by a cadre of new cooking tools ready for her immediate use.

A wide smile arose on Sarah's face and her eyes seemed to glisten. "Oh, Michael, what are those?" pointing to the new utensils.

"Well," Michael rubbed his bearded chin. "I figured you been use'n that old stuff we brought from Herkimer long enough. T'was time ya had som'thin new. So, me 'n the boy, we rode into town, to The Merchantile, 'n brung ya some new stuff." As Michael spoke he was carefully checking the condition of his boots. His face began to flush. 'Twere'nt no big deal, so don't be fussin."

George looked from his pa to his mother and back to his pa. He beamed with pride for what his father had done. It had been their little secret and they had kept it well. "Pa never spent nuthin' if he could help it," George later confided to his younger siblings. They had never seen anything like it before.

Realizing her husband didn't wish to spend another moment on the subject, Sarah continued her search through the new house. A sturdy loft hovered over a portion of the room, its plank floor providing ample sleeping area for her growing boys. Below the loft, a doorway opened into a large room that would serve as the girls' bedroom. It was beautiful and, oh, so necessary. The girls were getting older and really needed their privacy.

A smaller room with a separate entrance stood next to the girls' bedroom along the back half of the house. For the first time in the five years since they had left Herkimer, Michael and Sarah would enjoy the privacy of their own bedroom.

Sarah instantly loved their new home. She had not been particularly happy with Michael's decision to leave Herkimer. She would miss her mother and father. They were both getting older and she would much rather have continued living nearby. But, that wasn't hers to decide. She knew her role as his wife. It was to support his efforts, provide him with children so he could run a productive farm, and raise their family to be healthy, respectful and supportive of his work. At the age of 37, she had now given Michael ten children. Another would soon be arriving.

This home was his gift back to her. She saw his love in the sturdiness of the house he had built, in the beautiful hearth with all its new cookware, in the extra little things he had done to add comfort. Michael was a good and successful farmer. He was also a good husband and father. What more could she ask?

# The Arrival

Jessie and Rosie looked around the room as House lapsed into a temporary silence.

"Well, I suppose I get the idea", Jessie quipped. "Of course, the rooms are so different now. The loft is gone . . . and the hearth."

Rosie stood up, walked over to the 6x8 alcove and laid her hand on one of the walls. "I think I can imagine Sarah preparing a meal here." She looked back as if their storyteller was sitting next to them near the potbellied stove. "Where did you say the table was, Mr. House?"

"I didn't, but . . ."

"You know," Jessie interrupted, "if we're going to have this conversation, you need to have a name. 'Mr. House' just doesn't cut it for me"

"I never really thought about that possibility," House murmured.

"How about Chuck or Jerry or Sid?" Jessie teased.

48

House didn't realize she was teasing him when he replied. "I don't really like the name Chuck. Makes me think of what Rosie's been doing with that pile of wood. You know, chucking it into the fire. – And Jerry? No. There was a Jerry here once. Nice kid, but . . . now, Sid? That's cool. But, naw. I don't think so."

Just to give him a hard time, Jessie sat straight up, and with a smug look on her face, added, "I know. Sparkie."

"Heavens, no!"

House actually shuddered until the windows began to rattle. "Makes me think of fire, the kind that would burn down an old building like me."

Sensing how much this last suggestion disturbed House, Rosie rolled her eyes and interceded with an idea of her own. "What about Arthur? It suggests strength, like the legendary King Arthur. Like King Arthur, you offer protection to the people under your roof. You're doing that right now."

House hummed.

"Now, I like that. . . . Arthur – Yes, I like that."

"Okay, Artie," Jessie snapped. "So, tell us more."

*     *     *

It was a frigid February morning. Sarah bent over yesterday's smoldering coals to rekindle the fire. Michael and the oldest three boys had already left the house to tend to the animals and would be expecting a hearty breakfast

49

when the milking was done. She stepped back as a small flame popped up from the tinder and a sudden sharp pain sped across her belly. Flinching, she stroked the baby inside, in part to acknowledge its presence, but also to find relief from her first contraction.

"Okay, so today's the day. Here we go again."

"Mother?" Mary, Sarah's eldest daughter, had silently drawn next to her. She placed a hand on her mother's shoulder. "Are you all right?"

Sarah turned, sporting a weak smile and whispered, "Go call your Pa, Mary. He'll need to get the midwife. This here baby is ready to come today."

Nancy, lived just a mile down the road. She was a dear friend and, though never officially trained as such, had considerable experience as a midwife. She and her husband had lived in the area for thirty years. Several families in this part of Ashford had recommended her to Sarah.

As Mary turned, she looked up at the loft where eight-year-old William was just beginning to stir. "Billy, get up and fetch your pa. Mother's going to have her baby today."

William sprang into action. It wasn't often he was called on for something important and he was delighted to be included. He laced his boots, tumbled down the ladder and scurried out the door. "Pa! – PA!"

Michael's face appeared in a paneless window of the shed where the men were putting the finishing touches on morning chores.

50

"What in tarnation's got into you, Boy? Stop yer yellin' before you scare all the animals."

In his excitement to reach his father, William plunged into a deep drift at the edge of the house and buried himself in the snow. When he reappeared his father was laughing. But the sparkle in his eyes was wiped away by his son's next message.

"Ma's havin' the baby."

Michael knew the drill. This being their eleventh child, one would think he wouldn't get so nerved up. But, whenever Sarah went into labor, well, Michael never quite got used to it. Clearing his throat, he looked over his shoulder. "Simon, you 'nd George finish up here. Conrad, help me hitch up the horses. Yer Ma's fixin' ta have a new baby 'nd I needs ta git Nancy."

It wasn't long before he was back with the midwife. Nancy didn't waste a minute. She climbed down from the wagon, crossed the snow-covered yard and opened the house door.

Sarah looked up from the wash tub in front of her, her face flushed from wringing out one of Michael's shirts.

"Sarah, what *are* you doing?"

In a weak, almost shaky voice, she replied, "I was just finishing up some laundry."

At that, she pulled herself off the floor, reached for the wash board she had been using, and leaned over to put it away. A muffled gasp escaped and she grabbed at the wall to steady herself during the next contraction. Nancy wisely waited a moment, but when the pain seemed to subside, she ordered Sarah into her bedroom.

Meanwhile, Michael stared at the scene through the open door. Shaking his head, he mumbled something about "...that woman." Then, knowing full well he would not be welcome in the house until after the baby arrived, he turned to the boys who had already been sent outside. They stood huddled in the cold waiting for their father. "Where we gunna go, Pa?" George moaned. "We can't just stand out here, can we?"

"Come with me, boys. I be lightin' up the old potbellied stove in the shed. Got some hot cocoa. That'll warm up yer inners."

So, while the women went about the business of preparing for the new baby, all the men, big and little, gathered around a roaring hot fire not too far away. Michael told stories about life along the Mohawk River in Central New York and the boys pried him with questions about new babies.

"Michael – MICHAEL!"

It had been several hours since the midwife had arrived. Chatter in the shed had turned into an uncomfortable silence and the boys, one by one, had found some simple activity to keep them busy. Michael was nervous. He was having a hard time sitting still but had just closed his eyes trying to relax. The urgent call from the house brought him to his feet and got his full attention.

"Michael, go get Dr. Wilson. Sarah's baby is all wrong fer comin' out. She's going to be in a heap of trouble if he doesn't get here soon."

Dr. Abram Wilson, a graduate of Geneva Medical School in 1848, had moved into the area shortly after commencement exercises. His practice already had a proper reputation. Though a mere three miles away, it would not be an easy ride. The snow was deep and treacherous. As he mounted, Michael assured his boys, "Be back with Doc Wilson sooner 'en you kin shake a stick."

When the doctor finally arrived, Sarah's daughters collectively gathered around him. Shaken by an apparent problem that could affect their mother's health, some expressed dismay over the situation. The younger ones remained silent and seemed more in awe. They had never seen a real doctor before. What magic could he perform that the midwife had not done herself?

Dr. Wilson was well aware most women preferred a neighborhood midwife to the presence of a male doctor when it came time for the baby to arrive. He also realized his next words would not please the girls, and a pained expression overshadowed his initial smile. "I think it might be best for everyone to just leave our friend, Nancy, and me to talk in private." The look of disappointment in Mary's eyes caused him to partially reconsider and he added, ". . . but, Mary, please join us." As the rest of the young women began to find other ways to occupy themselves, the young doctor looked straight into Nancy's eyes. "Now, tell me what's happening."

"The pain started early this morning," Nancy began. "It's been going on for about six hours now." She paused and looked at Mary as if for reassurance. "This is Sarah's eleventh child and she told me none has taken so long in the past. She said the baby feels different, like its kick is not right."

The doctor nodded in response. "Well, let's take a moment to talk with Sarah. Won't you join me, Nancy?"

As he lifted the latch of the bedroom door and looked in, Sarah turned toward him, a worried expression on her face. Though the good doctor could tell she was searching for an answer, for the moment he only had questions.

A few minutes later, the girls watched as Nancy re-entered the family's living space. Though she didn't appear distressed, they noticed a somewhat puzzled look in her eyes. She headed directly for Sarah's rocking chair, picked it up like it was a feather, and carried it into the bedroom without a word.

Another several minutes passed before the door opened again. As the doctor re-entered the room, Mary looked straight at him. Her eyes met his and challenged him to offer some explanation . . . anything that would set aside their rising fears. Dr. Wilson nodded and smiled to acknowledge her as he sat down.

"You need not worry, ladies. I have no doubt your mother will be fine. Right now, your mother and your brand new little one are getting to know each other in a special way. The baby has turned around and can't figure out how to get out. Your mother is now rocking in her favorite chair. That will calm both your mother and the baby. In an hour or so the child will turn around all by itself. Then it will be able to join us in the world."

Standing, he walked to the hearth and poured himself a cup of steaming hot coffee. Then he slipped on his coat and hat, and headed for the front door. Several of the women watched with an obvious question in their eyes. As he opened the door, he looked back and smiled. "I'm sure your father would like to know what's going on, too. I'll be back in a moment."

Time passed while Sarah gently rocked and hummed to her child. Eyes closed, she thought about the new life in her belly and about all that had occurred while it was growing. The trials of raising so many children, the fact that Michael had been away for nearly a month while he finished building their new home, the move itself, and all the work of settling into this wonderful house. No wonder the baby had turned around and was anxious. A maternal calm cast a warm and cozy blanket over mother and child, and the baby turned, now ready to leave its watery home of the last nine months.

A sudden gasp escaped Sarah's lips as the baby began its journey to the world outside. Dr. Wilson, who appeared to have dozed off, sat straight up at the muffled sound coming from behind the bedroom door. In an instant he was on his feet and had entered the room.

"Nancy, come join me. Mary, you should come too. You're old enough to learn about birthing."

Sarah paled and held her breath as another pain came and went. She had done this before. She could do it again. The pain, though intense, was an announcement of a new life about to arrive.

It wasn't long before Michael heard the lusty cry of a newborn. He waited and watched, at the same time both wishing he could be standing next to Sarah, and relieved that he wasn't. Finally, four of his five daughters streamed out the door, coatless and mindless of the cold air and the snow.

"Papa, Papa!," they cried nearly in unison. "Mama just had a baby boy. Come and see. Come and see him."

As Michael entered the house, the doctor was reaching for his coat. "Well, Michael, I see the girls have already announced the arrival of your new son. He's a big one. Another set of hands to help on the farm."

"We'll be callin' him, 'Jacob'," Michael announced through a wide smile. "I'll be thankin' ya fer yer fine services, Doc. Money's a might thin right now. So, if it suits you, I'll be sendin' over a pig fer yer use."

At that, the two men shook hands and Dr. Wilson headed for home.

# Knight in Shining Armor

Jessie and Rosie sat mesmerized by the tale of Jacob's birth. Rosie broke the silence. "What was it like for you, Mr. House – I mean, Arthur?"

Arthur remained quiet for a moment. He was reveling in the sound of his new name. Arthur. . . . It meant strength and protection, two great qualities for a house to possess.

"I was thrilled. Imagine, a tiny little baby in the house. The whole scene was pretty exciting. To me, the midwife seemed to know what she was doing. As the hours passed, though, it became clear the situation was beyond her abilities. I give her credit, though. It couldn't have been easy to turn this over to a doctor. For centuries, birthing had been a midwife's domain. The field of medicine in the mid 1800's was just getting past the practice of purging. She must have known from some earlier experience that Dr. Wilson was part of a new era of medicine."

57

"I know this is way off the subject," Jessie chimed in, "but, I was wondering, how did Michael pay for all this stuff? You know, the new house, and didn't you say when they arrived they had just one cow?"

Arthur thought for a minute, then told them about Michael's visit to the bank.

*     *     *

As winter storms came to an end, Michael knew it was time to take the next big step in his plan; more cows, a litter of pigs and a hen house filled with chickens laying dozens of eggs. These were a must if the family was to succeed. So far, their livelihood had been based on his cousin's generous gift of a temporary house and a good deal of old time bartering. Michael knew, though, they needed cash to purchase the number of service animals he would need for his new farm. He could no longer put off a trip to the bank.

It was an overcast day, the heavy clouds threatening snow as Michael hitched the wagon for the ride to town. With a sigh, he climbed aboard hopeful of a successful journey.

"Git up, Babe."

Hunched over to ward off the cold, Michael never looked back to see Sarah waving and watching as she prayed for a safe journey and for success at the bank. For the next two hours he watched his horse's tail as it swished back and forth. Michael took full advantage of the quiet time to plan his request and practice his plea.

A gentle blast of warm air met Michael as he opened the door of The First National Bank of Springville. It wasn't his first visit, but it certainly was the most important. Walking to the edge of the lobby, where a narrow gated railing separated the ins and outs of many customers from the bank officers, he stood and waited to be seen.

"Well, good morning." A short bespeckled and slightly balding man looked up from his desk. "What brings you to town on this frosty day?"

Michael, usually sure of himself, suddenly felt like he'd rather be any place but here. It seemed like all the words he had carefully practiced on his way to town had stayed on the front seat of the wagon now hitched to a post on the other side of the door.

Mr. Leland recognized an all-to-familiar glaze in Michael's eyes and realized his potential customer was about to panic. He stood up, moved to the railing and extended his own hand in welcome.

"I can tell you have a lot on your mind today. Come and sit. Would you like a cup of coffee to warm yourself?"

The friendly greeting and kind offer of the bank officer were enough to help Michael relax a bit. "Don't mind if I do, Mr. Leland. Maybe just a bit o' cream."

As the bank's vice president delivered a steaming cup of fresh brewed coffee and walked back to his armchair, Michael wrapped his hands around the mug. The warmth soaked into his fingers and the words he had practiced started coming back to him. "Me 'nd the wife, we got us a piece o' land the other side of the creek. Gonna need some cash to build up my herd. I was wonderin' if I could get me a loan." There. It was out. Michael took a long slow sip of coffee to steady himself.

"I see, and how many acres did you purchase?"

"Fifty four acres o' rollin' country. Got a stream runnin' through it 'nd some open land good fer grazin'. Got me two good milkers now; figure I needs' maybe three or four more to make a living."

For the next several minutes the two men bantered back and forth while the banker learned about Michael and his plan. "

L.R.Smith runs a cheese factory just down the road a piece," Michael offered. "Tells me he's lookin' fer more farmers ta bring milk."

"Yes." the banker responded. "I know the man. It's a small operation, but he seems to be doing a good amount of business."

"What don't go ta Smith," Michael added as if he didn't even hear the banker, I plan ta churn into butter." He paused and his eyes brightened with another thought. "Got plenty o' maple trees on my land. I figure the sugarin' should be profitable."

As the two carried on their conversation, Michael could see Mr. Leland's head nod with a satisfied look. In the end, he walked out to his wagon with a firm promise from the banker of considerable support. Paying off the line of credit, he knew, would be a worrisome burden, but he felt confident he would be able to keep his end of the bargain.

*     *     *

Now it was Arthur who wanted to change the subject.

"There was somebody else who showed up at Michael and Sarah's farm. It was a few months after Jacob was born. I'd like to tell you about him."

"Who's that?" Jessie raised an eyebrow, though she grabbed for her pencil again, ready to log the details of another story.

"Out of the blue one day, a young man by the name of Matthew showed up. He sure did stir up the older girls. I remember his visit like it was only yesterday."

*     *     *

"Hey, Pa. There's a fella out here." Conrad stuck his head into the shed doorway. "Says he wants to talk to ya. Somethin' about makin' shoes for us."

Michael put down the scythe he was sharpening and stepped out to greet the visitor. The young man, perhaps in his mid-twenties, clean cut with the start of a beard was sitting on a horse. He had a bright smile and an earnest look about him.

"Mornin'. What brings ya out here on this fine day?"

As Michael conversed with the stranger, out of the corner of his eye he spotted two of his daughters, now young women, peeking out from the house. He smiled, quite sure of what they were thinking.

A moment later he saw Nancy come out the door and stand on the front stoop. She couldn't take her eyes off the handsome rider. It was as if King Arthur's Knight had come riding in on his faithful steed. As the two conversed, Michael pointed toward the house.

"You stroll on up ta the house. I be right behind ya. Got a couple of things ta put away."

As soon as Nancy saw the stranger coming her way, she turned to leave and tripped on a chunk of stray firewood. Flat on her face, she could hear his hurried footsteps coming toward her. She didn't dare look up.

Gently, Matthew touched her arm. "Please. Allow me to help you up. Are you all right?"

The husky male voice made her all the more embarrassed and she buried her head deeper into her shaky hands.

"Please, Miss, take my hand."

At that, Catherine, spoke up from the front doorway. "Oh, Nancy's okay. She just doesn't want you to see what a silly nitwit she is. Please do come in. Father's on his way to the house now. …Can I get you a cup of water?"

Nancy's world crumbled as the handsome man leaned down one more time.

"Just go," she pleaded without looking up. "Just do what she says."

She was relieved she didn't have to face him and hated Catherine for intervening.

When Michael entered the house there was a twinkle in his eyes. "You seem to have impressed my daughters, Matthew." He looked around the room for Nancy, but she was nowhere to be seen. Mary and Catherine were trying to look busy without leaving the area. Eight year old Lavina and seven year old Sarah simply stared at the stranger in their midst.

"Sarah, Matthew here tells me he's a cobbler. Come ta see what we might be needin' fer shoes before winter sets in. I figure we can keep him busy fer a day or so."

Matthew, meanwhile, kept his eyes from wandering to the pretty young women who were eyeing him back. Surrounded by ten children of all ages, it looked like this stop on his journey across the farmlands of Western New York would be both profitable and enjoyable. His smile widened and he stood a bit taller as he tried to straighten his shirt.

Sarah gave her husband a quick glance and, seeing him nod his head, took immediate control of the situation.

"Off with you, children. Go find your shoes and bring them for this man to see."

One by one, for the next several minutes, each of the children stood before the handsome stranger while he checked the condition of their shoes and measured their feet. His gentle touch brought on muffled giggles from the girls as each tried to gain just a tiny bit of his favor and attention. Meanwhile, Simon, George and Conrad, more fascinated by the tools and materials than the man, kept him busy answering their questions. William and Herman, too young to understand what was happening, just followed the actions of their big brothers.

Michael stood back and watched. Every now and then he questioned the young cobbler.

"Can ya fix that one with a patch so's we kin pass'er down the line? All of 'm don't need new ones, ya know." From previous years, he knew this would be an expensive day.

When the older three boys were finished with their portion of the friendly foot inquisition, Michael sent them off to carry on the day's business.

"I'm thinkin' the horse stalls and pigsty need cleanin' today, boys."

As they were leaving, everyone could hear the three argue over who would do what. Raising an eyebrow, Michael started to turn, ready to step in, but then stopped himself. The boys could fight it out among themselves.

Simon headed for the horse stalls. "I'll get the horses. You guys take care of the pigs." He knew better than to look back.

"That's just great," George complained. "We're stuck with the pigs again."

"Yea, well, this time let's try to keep them away from us until we're done."

"Sure. Good luck with that."

For the next half hour, the two boys shoveled and carried away the pigs' muck. The whole job was going quite well until one of the pigs decided he needed to poop and the boys were standing right where he usually did it. With a snort, the pig pushed his way past the flimsy barrier the boys had built and plowed his way toward the boys.

"Hey! Stop right there." Conrad yelled as if his words would do any good. He slammed down his shovel, but the surprised pig dodged it and ran directly into George.

"Yowee!" George landed flat on his back in the middle of the muck. When Conrad saw that, he began laughing. He laughed so hard he never saw George pitch his shovel at him. Too late, he tried to avoid falling, but instead, landed in a heap alongside his brother.

Hearing all the commotion Michael moseyed on down to the pigsty and found his boys wallowing in the pigs' muck.

"Best you boys go on down to the creek and wallow in there for a while. Your ma's gonna be none too happy if'n she sees ya like this."

Then, calling to Simon, he told him, "The horses kin wait till tomorrow. Git yerself down here 'nd clean up this mess yer brothers been making." At that, Michael returned to the house and assured the women folk all was well with the boys.

By the end of the day, Matthew's efforts stood lined up against the wall. Some would have new shoes, some hand-me-downs. From a supply of tanned cow hides he kept in his saddlebag, he had assembled or patched several

65

pairs of boots and shoes that would keep the family warm and dry throughout the year.

Michael put a hand on the cobbler's shoulder and nodded. "Come with me, son. I keep some cow hide in the shed that ya might be usin'. Just might cover part o' the payment." When they returned to the house, Matthew carried a wide grin on his face. In addition, the clink of a few coins sounded from his pocket.

Sarah, too, rewarded his efforts that evening with a sumptuous dinner accompanied by tall glasses of switchel, and topped off the meal with fresh blackberry cobblers.

"This sure was a fine meal, Ma'am," Matt wiped the last trace of cobbler from his mouth. "Maybe the best blackberry cobbler I've ever had."

"Picked 'em up near the top of the hill," Simon offered. "We found a big ol' patch of bramble bushes up there this summer, an' we cleaned 'em out. Ma's got plenty more down in the cellar."

Michael leaned back and surveyed the way his brood had taken to this young traveler. "Matthew." He held his eyes on the cobbler for a moment. "There be a Huskin' Bee down the road a piece tonight. We'd be right happy ta have you join us there." Then he looked at his pretty daughters. "Give the girls a chance ta fuss over ya – it would. After it's over, ya kin stay the night here by the hearth before ya carry on with yer business in the mornin'."

When Michael and the family pulled up to the cornfield with a good looking young man in the wagon, neighbors turned their heads. Later, though, when they saw that Matthew pitched in and did his part, everyone accepted him with an encouraging word and a smile. Moving through row upon row of corn stalks, the neighbors bantered and joked and told tall tales of achievement, too often hard to believe.

Well into the night, when the corn was all husked and ready for the mill, work turned into a neighborhood social gathering. One of the neighbors pulled out his accordion, and Michael, Sarah and the entire family, along with their young guest, joined in the singing. Matthew took turns dancing with Mary, Catherine and Nancy while the younger children made faces and teased their happy sisters. Then, much, much too late into the night, when the music was over and the treats and cider were nearly consumed, one by one, tired families hitched up their rigs and headed home.

The next morning, Nancy stood watching from the window. She was happy. In spite of an embarrassing start, the young peddler had given her a bit more attention than her siblings, or so it seemed. After the previous day, she watched him ride off like a knight in shining armor.

# The Hunt

Rosie stretched and, in spite of her interest, let out a big yawn.

"What a fascinating time that was. If that was today, we'd just go to Walmart and pull a box of shoes off the shelves."

"Yea, I've seen those boxes," Arthur replied. "Gee, I wonder what the city is like. Life must be a lot easier there than out here in the country."

"Well, I have to admit," Jessie chimed in, "I prefer the lights and action of the big city, but it's not half bad out here. Rosie and I have been having a ball traveling the area in search of her Native American roots."

"Did you say action, Jessie?" Arthur sounded excited. "I'll give you action. Let me tell you about Michael's run-in with a cougar back in '55 – that's 1855, by the way."

*       *       *

The scream of a cougar pierced the midnight silence. It wasn't the mournful call of a male for his mate, but the menacing announcement of a predator ready for the kill. Michael stirred and rolled over, uneasy with what he had just heard. Native to the area, the cougar's call was not at all unfamiliar. Tonight, though, the cat was simply on the prowl, or so he thought. Killing time was usually quiet and swift. The sound would come from the hunted, not the hunter.

Besides, Michael didn't really want to leave the warmth of his bed. It had been a long and difficult winter. To top that off, the area was now in its second day of a severe winter blast, a Nor'easter. A blanket of snowflakes swirled outside his bedroom window. It came in waves, sometimes causing a complete whiteout, sometimes drifting down like from a sieve. But, for two days, it had not stopped.

Michael knew from bitter experience that, before this was over, the wind would cast the flakes into deep drifts that would make life miserable for man and beast. He had spent the entire previous day dealing with the snow and the wind and the cold. The livestock, though not under cover of a building, had been gathered and now huddled under the protective eaves of a long shed where Sarah tended to her chickens and Michael kept his equipment.

Suddenly, somewhere in the darkness, the cat found its prey. A snarl, a flurry of noise from frightened cattle and the sound only a dying animal can make told Michael he had thought wrong. There was no use getting up now, but he dreaded what the morning would bring.

The family awoke to a sea of fresh whiteness as the sun rose over the crest of the hill at the front of the house. The storm had passed. It left a severe but beautiful picture with trees painted white on one side and deep clean drifts encircling the house. Not one footprint broke the entire Artic-like surface. Michael and the boys groaned at the sight.

Today would not be a normal day. Today, the young ones would not be trudging off to the schoolhouse only a mile down the road. Today, everyone in the area would be digging out from the storm and rescuing their cattle to keep them from freezing in the bitter winter weather.

Conrad was the first out the door. He loved winter and smiled as he breathed in the crisp fresh air. Strapping on his snowshoes, he made straight for the place where his father's ox, nine cows and five horses huddled in the shelter offered at the back of the shed. He, too, had heard the nighttime commotion and he was anxious to see what had taken place. What he saw when he arrived, though, was worse, much worse, than he had expected. The smell of fresh blood met him as he rounded the corner of the shed. Gaping at the gory scene before him, he was forced to turn away.

"Pa!" He willed his voice to stop shaking. "Pa, ya need ta git out here."

With a long, low sigh, Michael shook his head and looked at his wife with eyes that spoke a mixture of anger and sadness. Then he strapped on his snowshoes and left the house on his way to the scene of the crime.

A trail of blood mixed with fresh snow led to a nearby spot where the cat had dragged the young heifer and feasted. Entrails lay scattered at the base of a tall elm tree. Michael noted that the feast must have lasted until after the storm had passed. Clear but bloodied tracks led away from the remaining carcass into the woods.

"Conrad, git my gun and hunting knife and a handful of shot. I gotta git this critter before it gets hungry again."

Armed with his hunting equipment and a large piece of cornbread Sarah had provided to ward off the cold, Michael began to follow the cat's tracks. They led him up the hill and across the meadow. The deep snow left a clear path as the cat moved toward high ground and the thick forest ahead.

As Michael left the meadow to enter the dense growth of forest, a momentary movement on his right side caught his attention. Swinging in that direction, he raised his carbine to his shoulder but saw nothing. Eyes trained to ferret out the slightest change in environment scanned the area. Still, nothing. He eased the weapon down from his shoulder and prepared to move on. Again, a shadow of movement grazed across his field of vision. A chill ran down his spine, not from the icy cold, but from a keen sense of someone or something present.

71

"Who goes?"

His voice was low, but clear. Only silence responded. Michael was too experienced to ignore what he felt.

"I say, who goes?"

This time the call was clearer, firmer, more demanding of an answer. The inner person in Michael nearly died of fright as a man with a bow and a sheath of arrows rose from behind a patch of brush not ten yards away from him. The native, a man of possibly thirty years, wore a plain blanket cloth overcoat that hung nearly to his knees. His head, hairless except for a small tuft at the crown, was unprotected. A thin band of cloth from which two feathers aimed downward was tied around it. His hands appeared protected by gloves that left his fingers exposed to the winter's cold.

Struggling to maintain his composure, Michael spoke.

"You startled me, friend. What brings you to these parts?"

The man stood straight and silent for a moment before speaking.

"My people are hungry. The winter is long and hard. I come to our old hunting grounds where I know there are many deer. I do not want to bother the white man, but I need food for my people."

Inside, Michael breathed a sigh of relief. He lowered his weapon and smiled. "I be lookin' fer a cat that killed my heifer last night. Go find yer deer. There be a big herd in these here parts . . . and, God be with ya."

At that he turned and again began following the cougar's tracks. From the corner of his eye he saw the stranger fade into the woodland and disappear.

Soon, Michael entered a wide shallow gully. The snow lay thick and without blemish, save the tracks of a variety of small animals and, of course, the cougar's trail. The tracks he followed crossed to the other side, straight into a patch of bramble bushes. Behind them lay a small area of thick underbrush. From where he was standing, Michael could see no evidence of tracks leading out of the bushes. It seemed a perfect spot for the cat to rest after its feast. Ready to confront his four-footed enemy, he advanced on the cat with a slight breeze in his face. Meanwhile, the cougar slept, satisfied and unaware of his presence.

Finally, Michael's well-trained eyes spotted the sleeping animal. He stopped, raised the rifle to his shoulder, cocked the hammer without a sound, and fingered the trigger. A flash exploded from the end of his barrel and the sound shattered the quietness of the moment. In the thicket, the cat screamed and leaped into the air, twisting and turning in pain. It landed and, with a vicious snarl, tore out of the undergrowth to confront its enemy. As Michael reloaded – pushing a new ball into the breech – cocking the hammer – the injured cat was fast approaching. Again, Michael took aim and fired. The ball whizzed past the cat and pierced the thicket beyond.

Michael now knew he was in deep trouble. The carbine would now be useless as there was no time for a third shot. Dropping the gun, he took a deep breath and unsheathed his knife in a move that looked like he'd spent hours practicing. The knife sported a long polished blade, sharp enough to stop the angry cat if he got lucky. With a firm grip on the leather handle, he moved into a crouch, planted his feet, and waited for the cat to spring. The sleek body he saw rushing toward him was nearly four feet long not counting the length of its tail. It weighed probably close to a hundred pounds and would certainly bring on some serious damage. Michael knew, in his heart, he would be lucky to get out of this situation alive.

The cat leaped toward Michael and Michael raised his knife ready to plunge it into the exposed chest. He had drawn a mental picture of the cat's most vulnerable organ, and he was prepared to deliver the knife into a spot between and a little behind the cat's outstretched front legs. He saw, but couldn't think about, the long claws that were ready to tear him to bits.

Suddenly a long straight arrow whipped through the air and plunged into the cat. The shaft pierced its heart, the arrow head partially exposed on the opposite side. Caught in midair, the cat fell still and dead at Michael's feet.

Stunned, Michael turned to face the man he had just met. His eyes spoke gratitude as his voice, calm and clear, announced, "I be grateful fer yur help. Ya saved my life." Then he sank to the ground. His hands shook as he replaced the knife in its holder.

Silence reigned for several minutes while Michael regained his composure. Then he pulled out the cornbread Sarah had given him and broke it in half. Looking up, he held it out for the Native's taking.

"My name is Michael."

The younger man hesitated while Michael continued to hold the cornbread up for him. Taking a step forward, he reached for the bread.

"Little Bear."

The two munched on the food as each looked at the other in a somewhat new light. Again, Michael broke the silence. "Don't know if cougar meat is to yer liken', but yer free ta cut her up if it please ya."

Little Bear glanced at the dead cat, then back at Michael. "This belongs to the white man. It preyed on one of his animals."

Michael waved him off. "I just needed ta make sure it didn't kill again. My family has enough. Take it if ya like." Michael hesitated then asked, "Where you be from?"

"My people live near the Allegheny River. Our forest once had many deer and other wild animals. Now we must travel many miles to bring our families meat."

While Little Bear began to gut the cougar, Michael stayed nearby and watched.

75

# Sugarin'

"It was probably about midafternoon when the family saw Michael come walking down the hillside. He didn't have the cat and they feared it may have gotten away. After he had a chance to sit down and warm up with a nice hot cup of Sarah's vegetable soup, he told them about the Seneca he had met and how this total stranger had saved his life."

"How did the family react to the fact that this man had left the reservation? Were they at all concerned?"

"Well, Rosie, as I recall, Michael gave his children a strong lesson about loving your neighbor, regardless of who or what they are. He said something like, 'Now, this man, he saved my life. I don't particular care if he be huntin' up there or not. The man needed food fer his family 'nd it ain't fer me ta tell 'em he can't leave the Reservation.

76

So there ya have it.' As far as Michael was concerned he had just made a friend for life."

Arthur waited a moment to let the girls absorb the tale about the cougar. Then he went on with his story.

\*       \*       \*

Soon enough, winter's chill began to subside and the sun hinted that spring was coming. The trees on area hillsides and in the valleys were beginning to wake up. As liquid life began to spread through tree trunks and limbs, young buds were ready to open and make room for the greenery of leaves. Before the buds and leaves came though, and before the winter's snowdrifts disappeared, area farmers began the task of collecting the trees' valuable sap and turning it into maple syrup.

It was a Sunday afternoon, a day of rest from the heavy work of the farm. One of the boys heard the sound of a horse and sleigh coming down the road and looked out the front window. He turned to his parents.

"Mr. and Mrs. Frank are commin' back from church, and it looks like they're stoppin'."

Michael stepped out into the air to greet their neighbor. Lawrence and Lydia had recently purchased adjacent property and were starting their own farm. In their late twenty's, they were a handsome couple. Lawrence tethered the horse to a nearby tree limb.

"Mornin' Michael."

He tipped his hat as he spotted Sarah coming out the door.

"Good day to you, Mrs."

As Lydia climbed out of the carriage and joined Sarah in the house, the two men stood outside and talked.

"Been thinkin'," Lawrence offered. "'Seems about time to start collectin'. Don't you think?"

Michael scratched his beard and looked across the road at the deep snow on the hillside. The warmth of the daytime sunlight and the chill of the night air were combining to make the sap run unusually well for this early in the season. It surely was maple syrup time.

"Probably right. Though it'll be tough runnin' the sleighs through all this the snow."

Lawrence was eager to begin and Michael certainly didn't want to discourage his enthusiasm.

"How 'bout you spread the word that we'll be startin' the fire in the sugar shanty along about Friday. That'll give everybody time to set their taps and begin collectin'."

Maple syruping was a difficult task, but at this time of year not much else could be done around the farm. It was a valuable commodity, too. With the generous stand of hardwood trees found in the area, the township produced 20,000 lbs. of syrup every year. It was a great substitute for the more expensive sugar cane from the South and it was a valuable cash crop. Once produced, local farmers stored it until the weather improved enough to allow shipping to the rest of the State or, sometimes, they sold it to peddlers in exchange for the goods they carried across the countryside.

For the next several days, Michael and Simon were busy plowing their way through the deep February snow to prepare the trees. With his hatchet, Michael sliced a V-shaped wedge through the bark of the tree trunk. Simon followed and pounded in a small wooden spout. Buckets, made by Henry Miller, a neighboring cooper, hung from the spouts and collected the liquid gold.

Michael raised one eyebrow and chuckled to himself as he watched George and Conrad fuss and fume to their mother about not being able to help with the syrupin'. Both were still attending school at the nearby one-room schoolhouse.

"Ain't no reason fer us ta be schoolin' when there's sugarin' ta be done," George moaned as Sarah prepared the children's lunches for the day.

"School is your job now, boys. Soon enough, you'll be wishing that was all you had to think about. Besides, from the way you're using the English language right now, it seems you have a bit more to learn before you're done with school."

Sarah looked up and winked at Michael. She was determined to provide her children with a proper education, and Michael, who could barely read or write, didn't at all disagree.

"But, Ma," Conrad chimed in, "Miss Cathy ain't but a couple of years older than us. There's nothin' more she knows ta teach us."

Michael finally spoke, having the last word on any particular subject. "Mind yer mother, boys. You 'nd the youngins need ta be gitten on yer way. It's a long cold walk to the schoolhouse."

It wasn't long before horse and ox drawn sleighs began arriving at the community sugaring site. Some farmers kept the fire alive while others stirred the thickening syrup with large wooden paddles. Though a single farmer might be able to accomplish the task by himself, every year the men made a pact and everyone contributed both product and time to the job of boiling down the sap.

*(Permission: Bradford, VT Hist. Soc., Larry Coffin, Pres.)*

In spite of the hard work, the men thoroughly enjoyed themselves over the course of the next six weeks. When caught up on their own lines, they might cut and draw wood for the fire. Since it took an average of 40 gallons of sap to make one gallon of syrup, a great deal of such wood would be needed. Chilled to the bone from the arduous task of collecting the sap, the warmth of the fire drew the men together and the annual activity became quite the social event.

Sometimes the fire would overcook the syrup and produce a sticky goo. No one was upset though. The batch would simply become a form of candy. Cold and hardened, it was a delicious sweet for the children, though a random cube might be popped into an adult mouth here and there.

When the season's end neared, the women began to gather. It was time to oversee a celebration. Everyone in the neighborhood looked forward to this end-of-winter party. The men negotiated to divide the product of their late winter effort while approving mothers discussed their children's future and the children played.

The days lengthened, the sun grew warmer and the season turned to spring. Winter's white drifts sank into the earth. April came, alternately providing the sun's warmth to draw up the green grass and rain from the heavens to nurture it upon its arrival; then May. With his equipment well-oiled and ready, Michael set his mind to the next important task of planting the fields. But the rain held him in check.

"This rain," he complained to Sarah, "is makin' the plantin' a big problem. If it don't stop soon, we just gonna get buried in mud out there."

And the rain kept coming.

Michael fussed and fumed, helpless to get underway. And, while he fussed, the creek in the valley behind the house poured over its banks and spread across the entire width of the valley. One soggy morning, after the milking was done, the cows had crossed the creek on their way out to pasture. Though the creek ran fast, it was not yet a problem. Now, with the afternoon sun waning, they were stranded. Ready to be milked, though unwilling to return. Raging and spilling over the rocks and brush that got in its way, the creek denied them access to their barn.

Michael could hear them bawling. Reluctant to send the boys out after them alone, he sighed and got up from his chair.

"Guess we'll have ta go round the long way on Scoby Road 'nd prod them ta cross. Come along, boys."

Simon knew the routine but George and Conrad looked bewildered.

"Pa, there ain't no way ta get them across that valley. What'ya gonna do?"

"Well, boys," He winked at Simon. "We can herd them back the long way down the road and hope they don't charge off in seven different directions – OR we kin watch'em swim." A faint smile appeared on his face as the two stared at him. "It ain't a pretty sight, 'nd they'll bawl and put up a fuss, but they'll make it across all right."

A few minutes later all four stood in the meadow looking down at the rushing water that separated them from their house. Under protest, the usually calm cows had entered the valley. Now, half emerged in water, their tails straight up in the air, they sounded their protest but forged on. As they scrambled out of the flooded valley, the herd made straight for the protection of their barn.

\*       \*       ` \*

As the rain let up, the fields began to dry and Michael was finally able to plant his crop of wheat and oats.

# Makin' Room

Sarah's boys were growing up. They ate more, took up more space and played rougher than ever. On one particularly rainy afternoon, when their work was done and all had assembled in the house, the boys began some typical horseplay. Normally, Sarah felt she could tolerate pretty much anything. Today, though, the commotion was more than she could endure.

Conrad was hanging like a trained ape off the edge of the loft where the boys slept. George was throwing Sarah's ball of freshly spun yarn to Simon. Simon, as often was the case, wasn't watching where he was going. These young men, highly responsible when it came to the care of their farm animals, were now acting downright irresponsible.

"Boys – Boys! What are you doing? If you don't stop, something is . . . "

A loud CRASH interrupted Sarah's complaint. As the ball of yarn sailed over Simon's head, he leaped into the air to catch it. With one hand on the captured yarn, he came down on top of Sarah's rocking chair and both boy and chair collided with the back wall of the house. Sarah's favorite picture, one given to her by her parents before leaving their Herkimer home, crashed to the floor in splinters.

"Stop it. Stop it this very minute."

Sarah shrieked at her eldest son as she watched her picture fly in several directions all at once.

"Look what you've done. Look at my beautiful picture."

Tears fell as she stood over Simon, ready to break any bone still intact in his youthful body.

At that, the front door opened and Michael stepped in. Bewildered by the scene taking place in front of him, he turned to his wife. Before he spoke though, he got his answer. Sarah was crying as she picked up the broken picture. She shook her head in dismay, then turned and stared at her husband.

"Lord knows, Michael, with eleven youngins in these cramped quarters, it's near impossible to keep order. I do what I can do, but somehow we need more space."

Michael had heard this line of thinking before, but never under circumstances like this. Afraid to look at his wife while in her present state of mind, he turned and reached for the doorknob.

"I'll be goin' now."

Not finished with her tirade, Sarah raised herself up to her full five feet, three inches.

"Don't you be leavin' now. Your son has just ruined my rocking chair and he shattered Mama's picture."

This brought Michael to a full stop. For just a moment he wished he had never walked in the door. Then, with a deep sigh, he turned back to the scene of the crime. In a low controlled voice he spoke to his boys.

"Simon – Conrad, git yer things 'nd come with me . . . 'nd bring yer ma's broken chair and the picture with ya. We got some fixin' ta do."

Without another word, he opened the door and retreated to the more peaceful environment of his own workshop. He much preferred the sound of the breeze whistling through the structure and the voices of his animals to the cross words and tears of his wife. He spent the rest of the day teaching the boys valuable lessons in self-control, communication with the women folk, and carpentry.

As suppertime approached, their lessons were interrupted by the sound of a bell. One of the boys closest to the window looked toward the house. His mother was standing at the front door rigorously sounding the family's dinner bell. Since the bell could be heard pretty much anywhere on the farm, this was her routine way of calling the family for a meal.

Upon entering the house, Michael watched his two guilty sons approach their mother bearing gifts.

"Ma," Simon started. He was holding a freshly built frame for the victimized picture. Sarah's eyes moved from son to son to picture. Then, wiping both hands on her apron, she whisked away a tear that appeared at the bottom of her right eye and hugged each boy in silence.

". . . I'm sorry." Simon said, finishing his apology.

*       *       *

A few days later, Sarah was busy cleaning up after a big breakfast of flapjacks with maple syrup and a side of pork when she heard the sound of a horse and cart. This wasn't unusual. The road was, after all, the main route between Springville and Ellicottville, the County seat. Today, though, it sounded like the driver might be stopping. She peeked out the window.

*Sure enough, he's stopping. Oh, here comes Michael. The man's getting out of his wagon. Wonder what that's all about.* She looked back toward the hearth. *Better put on a pot of coffee.*

It wasn't long before Michael brought this stranger into the house. The two stopped several steps short of the front door. First one, then the other pointed here, then there, seeming to discuss aspects of the house. Finally they entered.

"Sarah, this here is Daniel Cole. Daniel lives up on Dutch Hill. He's here to talk about buildin' on ta the house."

Sarah gave this stranger the once over. He was short, stocky and quite weathered. He looked like he had been around for a while; maybe 50ish. He had an honest face, she thought, and strong calloused hands.

"Good day, Mr. Cole. May I offer you some coffee?"

He smiled, a sincere smile she thought, as he settled down on one end of the dining bench and nodded in the affirmative.

"Don't mind if I do, Mrs."

"The wife here," Michael nodded in the direction of Sarah. "thinks we might be needin' a bigger house." With the slightest twinkle in his eye, he looked at Sarah. "Seems like my boys need a bit more room ta grow."

Sarah cocked her head. She knew he was teasing her, but also realized he was about to enter into some serious talk about building on to their home. Her smile grew.

"Sarah, Mr. Cole here, has quite a reputation fer helpin' people build houses. I thought you might be tellin' him what yer thinkin'."

Surprised by the gesture and a bit nervous, Sarah wiped her hands on her apron for what seemed the hundredth time. Fidgeting, she was unable to look directly at Mr. Cole, but began in a low voice.

"Well, Mr. Cole, this room is where I cook, where we live and, for the boys . . ." She looked up at their loft sleeping quarters. "well, it's where our six boys sleep. It's getting awful crowded, five of them being young men. The loft Michael built is good, and it's strong, but their growing bodies need more space."

She looked to her husband for any sign of disapproval, but found none. He nodded as if to say, "Yer doin' fine." Still watching her husband, she added, "Is it possible to have an actual kitchen and one of those wood burning stoves with the warming oven on top?" She looked deep into Michael's eyes. "When I was over at Nancy Frank's house, she showed me hers. It's a wonder what you can do with them." Not quite begging, she went on. "It would be so much easier than the hearth."

Michael looked at her pleading eyes and caved in. With the slightest nod, he let Daniel know a new kitchen was in order.

Three weeks passed. On his initial visit all had agreed to give Mr. Cole some time to put together a plan and an estimate of the cost. Except for one brief roadside conversation, they had heard nothing. The summer would soon be over and they grew concerned they might be spending another winter in their cramped quarters. Finally, one morning, Daniel arrived with the plans.

"I'm hoping," he said as he rolled out a large sheet of paper on the table, "You'll be likin' my ideas."

What lay in front of the couple was something more than a freehand sketch and less than an engineer's design. Both knew Mr. Cole was experienced in the construction of houses. Proof of his abilities could be seen around the countryside. The drawing would lead them through a productive conversation.

"You'll be needin' a two story addition ta make room for your boys, Michael. My own home has the look I've prepared for you. It has served me well and, no doubt, will work for your family. The downstairs part gives you a new parlor and a new bedroom for you and the Mrs. Your girls can have the two bedrooms you now use. As for your new kitchen, Sarah, with the hearth gone we can connect that new wood burning stove, the kind Mrs. Frank showed you. Your livin' space here," He nodded his head to indicate the room they now occupied. "will be pretty much the same, except we'll get rid of the loft when the boys move upstairs."

Sarah swallowed hard as she glanced up at her husband. The plan sounded wonderful. Would Michael approve? Much relieved, she saw Michael nodding his head and indicating that he, too, found it acceptable.

"Well, Mr. Cole, this here plan sure enough gives us more space. I reckon we'll all be likin' that." He paused and looked around the room. Then, with a slight nervous laugh, he added, "All this looks like it will come at a right handsome price. What do you have in mind?"

Sarah began to busy herself in an attempt to disappear. There were breakfast dishes to be cleaned, laundry to be washed, never ending things scattered here and there to be picked up. The boys were out searching the bramble patches for the season's last round of blackberries. The girls were tending to her vegetable garden.

Daniel pulled a small pad from his overall pocket and opened it. "No reason we can't use the timber on your land fer framin' the house. And, I took a look at yer foundation. Where did you say you got those stones? As fer the walls and roof, I think David Oyer's mill down toward Ashford Hollow will charge a better price than Scoby right now."

The two discussed how Cole might carry out this big project without seriously interfering with the current living quarters. Finally Daniel quoted his price. "All in all, Michael, we can do this job for $700.00."

Sarah had stayed within hearing distance of the two men and heard the price. Trying not to be obvious, she twisted her head just enough to peek at her husband. The look on his face, she thought, was somewhat dismayed.

"I gotta say, Mr. Cole, that be a pretty hefty sum. I'll have to sell off half my stock ta pay ya."

"Well, I thought about that, Michael, and I have an idea that might help us both. If you can spare one of your sons, he can be part of my crew and I won't have to hire a go'fer. Works with me full time on the project and, maybe, he gets an interest in the trade. If you're agreeable, I can reduce the price by $150.00."

"I like yer idea, but give me a few days ta speak to the wife. I'll be seein' if one of the boys is agreeable. They're gettin' to an age now, where they should have a say."

*       *       *

91

It wasn't long before Daniel and his crew, including Sarah's son, George, were digging out and hauling stones for a new foundation. They found and prepared long, straight tree trunks for sturdy floor beams, and laid up the new two story addition.

Sarah's beautiful hearth lay in the direct path of construction and Daniel began making threatening remarks about where and how Sarah might soon be cooking the family's meals. Then, one day, a wagon carrying her brand new wood burning stove, complete with overhead warming ovens, arrived at her doorstep. Just in time. Men appeared from behind the house and climbed down from ladders, making their way to help unload it.

"Watch out, Boys – mighty heavy," Cole chided. "Soon as we get this here hooked up, we can break down that hearth, though 'tis a mighty nice one 'nd I hate ta see it go."

This was a bitter-sweet moment for Sarah. She recalled the day her husband had presented this beautiful gift to her. She loved that hearth, but the wood stove, a modern convenience, would be so much easier. No regrets, just happy memories of the dinners she had prepared for the ones she loved.

As the project advanced, Nancy, now seventeen, took quite an interest in one of the workers. He was new to the area and she prodded her brother to find out more about him.

"Oh, you mean Henry?" George responded with a little twist of his upper lip showing his amusement. "Sure, give me some time. I'll see what I can find out."

Later that day, Nancy was churning butter out in the shed behind the house. It had been a busy morning for her and she looked a mess. Her dress was stained from weeding in the garden, her hair quite undone, and tiny beads of sweat were sliding down her cheekbones as she vigorously worked the milk into butter.

"Hey, Nancy. You in there?"

The shed door swung open as Nancy looked up from her work. Much to her dismay, in walked George, and with him the young man she somewhat fancied.

"Old man Cole said we could take a break, so I thought I'd introduce you to my new friend, Henry."

Nancy looked first at Henry, then at George. This wasn't exactly the way she pictured her first meeting with Henry. All she wanted to do was crawl into some little hole where no one could see her. Right now, though, that wasn't an option.

Henry was standing next to George, his hand in his pockets. He was tall, as tall as George, and had muscles any woman would appreciate. His close cropped hair was a bit stringy at the moment, but in this heat, that was to be expected. The smile on his face was only outshined by the dreamy glow coming from his sky blue eyes.

However embarrassed she felt at the moment, Nancy decided it was no time to shrink away.

"Well, good day to you, Henry. It's very nice to meet you."

"And a good day to you, Miss Nancy."

Henry had got a glimpse of this interesting girl from time to time as he worked on the house addition. He had seen her teasing her sisters and cavorting with her brothers. Too, he had watched her when she was working and saw that she was a hard worker. He liked what he saw and was happy George had introduced them.

"Henry, here, grew up not far from where we lived, Nancy."

Nancy gave George a look that told him to get lost. While she wasn't thrilled to meet under these circumstances, she had no intention of making this a three way conversation.

"So tell me, Henry, where are you from?"

Henry found an empty wooden barrel just about stool size, flipped it over, and sat down within touching distance of Nancy. "I grew up in Oneida County, a little place called Marshall."

George looked from one to the other, shook his head, winked at Nancy and left. Nancy didn't even see him leave.

"I know where Marshall is," she offered. "It's not that far from Herkimer where I grew up. What brings you to these parts?"

Henry leaned back against the wall and clasp his hands together behind his head. Nancy thought he looked pretty comfortable and kinda sexy.

"Well, I'm the oldest of six. The house was getting pretty crowded and, anyway, it was time to be moving on. I'm pretty good with a hammer and heard there was a lot of building going on in the western part of the State. So, I just decided to give it a try. Been here a year or so. What about you?"

Sarah noticed that Nancy was all atwitter that evening. The girl was obviously smitten by the young carpenter. "Michael, you'd better keep an eye on that boy," she warned. "He seems like a nice young man, but the way Nancy's talking, those two will be spending a lot of time together – if allowed."

# The Quilting Bee

Sarah marveled at the appearance of the house with its new second story addition. Daniel had trimmed the gables with matching cornice moldings on the left and right. A decorative crown over the new front door accompanied two matching recessed columns that stood guard on either side of the

*("Addition" by Patricia Iacuzzi)*

doorway and brought just a touch of class to their home. Handsome double hung windows, upstairs and down, allowed for easy entrance of morning sunbeams. The entire

96

house now showcased a handsome cedar clapboard exterior.

Inside, Sarah now had a new parlor as nice as the one she had left back in Herkimer. She and Michael shared a large new bedroom off the parlor, their old one now available for Catherine and Nancy. The new second floor would, forever more, be the domain of her boys, a potential disaster area to be avoided if at all possible.

Sarah's beautiful hearth was now just a memory. In its place, a handsome little nook offered her shelter where she made and mended a good deal of the family's clothing. It was just far enough out of the way that the boys' constant roughhousing would not interfere.

The family's original living space was still at the heart of their lives and activities. A portion had been converted to kitchen where Sarah's new stove was the main attraction. The oven more than compensated for the loss of her beautiful hearth. While the hearth once had been a delightful surprise and the source of many delicious meals, the new oven offered the potential for many new recipes she had in mind. An iron skillet replaced the stew pot as her primary cooking utensil. Baking bread would now be a breeze and the overhead warming oven would save many-a-meal when Michael was delayed by some unexpected problem.

Near the kitchen, a long table and benches invited the busy family to gather for meals and frequent evening board games. The boys' loft was gone, but Sarah's rocking chair still stood where she had seen it on that first day. She had always coveted that spot overlooking the ravine and was not about to lose it.

One day Sarah took a few minutes to relax. As she rocked in her favorite chair, she thought about all the changes that had taken place in the last few months. A far-away look covered her face as she stared out the window, too preoccupied to notice Nancy coming up behind her.

"Mother, are you okay?"

Startled, Sarah turned to look. She smiled as she studied her teenage daughter. No longer a mischievous, sometimes problem child, Nancy suddenly appeared very grown up.

"Are you thinking about Sarah, Mother?"

Sweet little Sarah had been taken ill just about a year ago. In spite of all their efforts, the nine year old had died. Surely it was just a common cold. Then her temperature skyrocketed, she began having uncontrollable chills and her cough raged with unrelenting severity. Upon examining her, Dr. Wilson announced the dreaded word - pneumonia. Nothing the doctor tried could conquer it. The loss for Michael and Sarah, for the entire family, had been devastating. This lively little girl was everyone's sweetheart. Good-tempered, generous, adventurous, always curious about the things that surrounded her, there was nothing about her not to love.

Nancy's innocent question bought all this back to Sarah. Reaching up, she touched Nancy's arm as a small tear traced a thin line down her cheek.

"Sarah will always be in my heart, dear. Her death was a tragedy, but the living must go on. Now, tell me, how goes it with young Henry?"

Nancy's mood brightened at the name of her beau. She wasn't sure if this was the best time to raise the topic, but Mother had asked. What could she do? A nervous cough escaped and she covered her mouth as she looked away for a moment.

"Well Mother, since you asked . . ."

Sarah turned to fully face her daughter. She noticed the sparkle in Nancy's eyes. She saw the way she smiled at the sound of Henry's name and the air of joy that suddenly surrounded her daughter.

"What, my child. What is it?"

"Mother—" Nancy was nearly bursting. "Henry and I have spoken of marriage. The next time he sees Father, he intends to ask for his permission to marry me."

For the moment, Sarah and Nancy were alone in the room. What happened next was an act of pure love between a mother and her offspring. Sarah stood up from her chair, turned and wrapped her arms around her child. Then, leaning back, she looked deep into Nancy's eyes and began to gently rake her fingers through her daughter's hair. Tears, this time of joy, again appeared as she spoke.

"I knew from the beginning he was the one. My dear, you two were surely meant for each other. You have my blessing and, while Henry will, of course, have to ask your father, I know you have his blessing as well."

At that, the front door opened and two of the boys barged in, deep in some petty argument. They never even saw Nancy glide away and disappear into her room.

*       *       *

"Michael, you and the boys will want to keep clear of the house this afternoon."

Sarah was busy cleaning up from lunch. She didn't look up as she spoke.

"I know. Yer havin' that quiltin' bee fer Nancy. Be a good time ta cut some wood. That'll keep the boys outa yer hair fer a while. They'll be comin' back with a whoppin' appetite though."

"Don't worry about that. We ladies will have a feast ready for you. You just make sure Henry comes back with you. Nancy will just die if he can't be here for the party."

Sarah watched Michael slip out the door as several friends and neighbors began arriving. This was the day everyone brought their special patch to complete a quilt, a gift for Nancy's wedding bed. It would be a prize possession in her trousseau.

Not long after her daughter's engagement was announced, Sarah had spoken to friends, asking for help. All had agreed and, one by one, each produced a square for Nancy's quilt. Today was the culmination of their efforts and a day to party. A quilting frame stood in the center of Sarah's new parlor. Eight women gathered around it to sew

100

in their patches, beautiful designs and intricate patterns made with great love for the new bride-to-be.

Today was also everyone's first opportunity to see the inside of Sarah's enlarged house. They all knew of Daniel's reputation for excellent workmanship and had been dying to see the results.

"Why, Sarah, this parlor is a sight to behold."

Sarah was delighted to hear what her friends had to say about the new structure.

As time passed, the women sewed, cut, stitched and assembled. Five-year-old Herman and tiny Jacob crawled under the frame to watch. A half dozen needles appeared, then turned around and disappeared as the women's hands swiftly brought the patches together. The latest gossip merrily traded places while the ladies caught up on neighborhood activities since their last gathering.

From behind the house, the women could hear the steady chopping of wood. They heard the sound of Michael's crosscut saw as it ripped through the larger tree trunks. Mixed in was the intermittent sound of someone splitting the wood into useable pieces. Every once in a while there would be no sound at all as the men rested or became engaged in some manly conversation.

Sarah stepped to the window midway through the afternoon and overheard a bit of their talk.

"Hey, Pa. Tell us again about that Seneca guy the day you went after the cougar."

Michael, who was engaged in splitting the wood, had just started a powerful swing of his ax. It landed with a resounding WHACK, and two chunks of wood flew in opposite directions. Satisfied, he turned to face the boys. A strange look overshadowed his face. His eyes widened and his voice grew serious.

"Boys, I was mighty concerned when he stood up behind that bush. Ya know, we don't 'spect ta meet them out there. . . . not in these parts. It was like I was alone, then I warn't."

"But, Pa, the reservation is miles south of here."

"Well, Little Bear, he didn't talk much, but when we was cuttin' up the cat, he tol' me 'bout them people."

Conrad gave his father a questioning look. "He still has a native name? In school, we heard that some are taking English names. . . . part of trying to fit in."

"Don't know much 'bout that, Conrad. All the same – said his name was Little Bear."

Michael leaned back against a nearby wall and looked off in the distance. "Ya know, they got it pretty hard down there. Can't say as I would be any too happy if somebody forced me ta change my way of living.

"When he tol' me his father brung him here when he was a lad, I asked if he knew 'bout that big boulder up in yonder valley. He said his father spent most part of one summer livin' near the boulder. Back then, I guess, the Native boys had ta go through some kinda initiation when they come of age. Anyway, the man had a run-in with a big ol' cougar back then, 'nd killed it. Took the name, 'Hears Like a Cat' after that when he come home."

102

Conrad looked about, his eyes filled with wonder, trying to catch sight of anyone who wasn't supposed to be there. "Maybe they come here more than we think."

At that, George, who was sitting out of Conrad's sight, chuckled and, with a devilish look, stripped off his shirt and crept up behind his brother. Finding a leaf, he picked it up and brushed it across the back of Conrad's neck, causing his brother to slap at it. As he did so, he turned and saw a bigger than life semi-naked figure only inches from his back. Startled, he nearly fell off the log. Everyone, except Conrad, thought the whole thing quite hilarious.

"Well, boys, this here Little Bear. He's a right nice fella. Told me he's learnin' a trade. Said if I ever needs ta build, I should git word 'nd he'll come ta help."

Michael stood, picked up the ax, and took a long look at the chunk of wood he was about to split. "Might be callin' on him ta build a new pen fer the pigs this summer." Then, he raised the ax and slammed it down, sending two more pieces in opposite directions.

Back in the house the quilt was now complete. The women traded recipes while they prepared a feast for the evening's meal. A quilting bee was an all-day event, a veritable day off from the tedious task of raising a family for the women, and party time for everyone when husbands and children of all ages gathered later. When the meal was complete and the dishes washed, dried and put away, a fiddle or two appeared and the room filled with music.

"Nancy, come dance with me."

103

Henry held out his hand to his bride-to-be. In a heartbeat, she sprang from where she sat on the floor and the two began a lively jig. Eleven-year-old Lavina giggled from the sidelines. Unable to contain herself, she leaned forward, looking for someone to grab. Her little brother, William, sat nearby. He, too, seemed excited by the music. Pulling him up, she dragged him to the center of the room where, together, they followed the actions of their big sister as best they could.

# Weddin' Time

"So, there's a wedding coming down the pike."

Jessie's eyes sparkled and a bemused smile lit up her face. She looked like she was ready to write the affair's delicious details in the next issue of the Springville Herald.

"I can see it all now, a real country hoe-down."

"Now hold on News Lady," Arthur countered. "I've got a feeling you are picturing a whole lot more than I've got to give."

At this point, Rose Mary leaned back against the wall, stretched out and crossed her feet. She was enjoying the banter between House and Reporter. Who knew this brief encounter with an empty house would be such fun, and useful too. Maybe she wasn't learning about her ancestors, but Arthur was laying out a pretty vivid picture of life around here in the 1800's.

Then there was Jessie. She was such a good friend and a really good reporter, but she . . . well, she had this tendency to jump to conclusions. Rosie had seen it happen before. In the end, though, Jessie always got it right. She was, without a doubt, a most interesting companion. Rosie never failed to appreciate her talent.

The voice from the room spoke again. "You have to remember, Jessie, these people were not high society. They were down-home country folk, raised and bred to be good farmers. Sure, marriage was a celebration, but more or less, it was simply passage into the next phase of a young couple's life.

\*       \*       \*

Nancy's wedding day finally arrived. Bright rays from a cheerful sun streamed over the eastern horizon while crisp sub-zero January air sent Nancy scrambling to get dressed when she got out of bed. A new layer of snow lay on top of two feet of white stuff already in place. But, all that didn't matter. Today was Nancy's day.

Through the closed door, Nancy could hear her mother already in the kitchen. The smell of coffee found its way into her room to announce that breakfast would soon be ready.

"Um-m-m, coffee today," she murmured. Coffee wasn't usually on the menu. It was far too expensive to indulge in on a regular basis. Maybe for Sunday, but never on Thursday. Then again, this wasn't your average Thursday. The preacher was coming today. Today she was going to marry Henry.

As she fastened the last button on her dress, Nancy heard her noisy brothers come tumbling into the house. Morning chores were over and, like any other day, the men were starving. A wistful smile appeared as she picked up her new mirror, a little gift from her father after a recent trip to the Merchantile in Springville.

"What a nice mirror Father has given me," Nancy whispered. "I will treasure this forever." With a satisfied glance at her reflection, she reached down, laid it back on the table and opened the door to join the family frenzy.

Breakfast was quick. Too much remained to be done before the guests would arrive. Mary, her sister, who had arrived the previous day, took control of kitchen duties along with Catherine, leaving their mother to assist Nancy. For the next hour, carriages and sleighs appeared and Simon, George and Conrad tended to the needs of their guests and cared for the teams. William and Jacob played host at the front door, took coats, and made the guests feel welcome with their antics.

As neighbors and friends entered the house, Michael and Sarah's new parlor became the center of attention. Everyone marveled at Daniel Cole's skilled workmanship. The addition, they all thought, was well suited to the needs of this large family.

Every inch of the parlor had been cleaned in preparation for the wedding. Windows were washed inside and out, surfaces clear of never-ending dust, and the floor had been coated with a fresh layer of paint. Sturdy benches assembled by Michael and the boys offered their guests a

107

place to rest as they waited for the celebration to begin. The growing pitch of conversations eventually forced each to overcome the voices of others until the room nearly rattled.

And Nancy waited. Behind the closed door of her bedroom, Nancy, her mother and all her sisters awaited the arrival of the groom.

"Is he here yet?"

Nancy couldn't understand the delay.

"I spoke to him yesterday. He should be here by now."

Sarah stroked her daughter's golden hair while she, herself, wondered.

"Never you mind, dear. He'll be coming soon enough."

Looking away, she turned to eleven-year -old Lavina.

"Go find your brothers, Lovi. Maybe they've heard something."

But, upon returning to her sister's side, Lovina could offer nothing further to ease their wonder.

The preacher waited, sitting in Sarah's rocking chair and staring at the mountain of January snow. The guests waited, little by little, growing silent as they ran out of useful conversation. Michael and the boys waited, eyeing the empty road that disappeared not far to the south into the January whiteness. Sarah waited, aware of her daughter's growing anxiety.

Finally Nancy stood up, brushed imaginary particles from the surface of her beautiful new dress, and stepped to the bedroom door.

"I just can't sit here anymore," she blurted as she twisted the handle with a nervous jerk.

As Nancy stepped out of the confines of her little bedroom, she saw the preacher look up at her. Before he could mask his souring mood she saw the annoyed look on his face, his piercing stare and fidgety movements, and she realized he was growing impatient. Embarrassed, she looked away, unable to face him. But, like he flipped a lever, he stood and came to her aid.

"What could be keeping young Henry, my dear?" His eyes softened and his voice grew tender.

"I don't know, Preacher. I'm so worried."

While Nancy was getting worried, a growing hint of anger was rising to the surface. She had heard of men who never showed up. Henry wouldn't do that to her. He wouldn't dare.

A trickle of guests began to rise from their seats. Reluctant women followed their husbands out of the parlor as they prepared to leave. The work of their farms called for a timely return and they could not wait any longer. Shuffling out, each avoided eye contact with the bride-to-be, and the busy house grew quiet. The only people left were the preacher, the family and a couple of young friends who had nothing better to do if they went home.

"Where is Henry?" Nancy directed the question to no one in particular. "I'll simply kill him when he gets here." Then, lowering her voice to almost a whisper, "Oh, I hope he's all right. I hope he's not hurt."

Finally, Simon slammed his fist on the table, stood up and announced, "I'm going to find him. If he's not dead or hurt, Nancy, I'll be the one do'in the killin'."

As Simon opened the door to carry out his mission, he spotted a man on a horse coming down the road. The horse was walking, almost limping. It was smeared with dried patches of dirt on its back, legs and hindquarter. Its rider appeared to be sporting a similar description.

"I'll be gol-derned if it isn't Henry. He's riding bareback on the horse and there's no carriage. Something must have happened."

The bedraggled young groom-to-be was none too happy. Forgetting about her fresh new dress, Nancy ran to him and wrapped her arms around him. The family and preacher watched in silence while the two touched and murmured and looked at each other. When Nancy finally pulled away, she stammered, "Whatever happened?"

"Crossing the creek . . . I thought the ice was firm enough . . . one carriage wheel broke through the ice. When the carriage frame hit the ice, it all gave way. I had all I could do to save myself . . . and the horse. Nancy, I'm sorry. We've lost our carriage . . . and, and I'm sorry I've made such a mess of things on our wedding day."

At that, Michael stepped forward.

"Well, son, we're just happy yer here. Now, you two go fix yer'selves up. The preacher, here, wants ta be on his way. Let's git this here marriage started."

On January 15, 1857, in the presence of their preacher and surrounded by their family, Henry and Nancy became one. Under the circumstances there was more than enough fruit cake to celebrate the occasion. While Nancy's brothers made the next hour a testing ground of the couple's endurance, Michael hitched up Henry's horse to a spare wagon and presented the result to the bride and groom.

"Now, ya be stayin' off the ice on yer way back to East Otto." he cautioned Henry with a broad smile on his face. "Nancy, here, prefers her bath just a mite warmer than the creek can offer."

# The Ride Home

Rosie and Jessie burst into a fit of laughter at Michael's warning.

"He really said that?" Rosie couldn't stop giggling.

"Yup. Nancy was mortified by her father's reference to her bath water, as was Sarah. When he saw them both glaring at him, he took a step back from the carriage. I remember his exact words before they left. Looking away, out toward the barn, he mumbled, "Now, git goin', before I git me in trouble with my own woman.""

"Oh, I just love weddings," Rosie mused. "I mean – well, you know." Suddenly embarrassed, she blushed. "I love the flowing white dresses, the bride's veil, and . . .""

"Oh, she wasn't wearing white. While that might have been the style in high society, out here in the country the women were way too practical to get married in a white dress. Around here the typical wedding dress doubled as an item of fine wear for some other big occasion.""

Jessie broke in. "So, do you remember what Nancy was wearing?"

"Like it was yesterday." Arthur was silent for a moment. "I was so happy for Nancy. She and Henry stood there in front of the preacher in the new front parlor. She was wearing a green floor length dress of form-fitting poplin over a brocaded skirt. A beautiful gold locket, an heirloom gift from her mother's mother, set off a high collar. The only white that was evident was her veil and a pair of white gloves.

"In contrast, Henry stood at her side wearing what must have been a brand new brown suit with a button-down vest. Only the suit was wrinkled and stained. The knees and elbows had big scuff marks from his ordeal in the creek." Arthur sighed. "They were a sight to behold, but both were happy. That's what is most important, isn't it?"

"Life got back to normal pretty fast." Arthur went on. "Soon enough signs of spring were popping up everywhere. One April morning Sarah got some news that brought clouds into her life in spite of the season.

*　　*　　*

Most Tuesdays and Fridays the postal delivery man trotted by and just waved. Sarah had resigned herself to the fact that she seldom got news from her family in Herkimer. Today, though, the carrier reined in his horse and waited for someone to come out.

"Mornin' Sarah. Got a letter here for you."

113

Sarah let out a tiny gasp, wiped her hands on her dress and reached up. With scarcely a word, she took the envelope from the carrier's hands, turned, and walked into the house.

As she walked away, the carrier mumbled, "Hope things is okay in Herkimer." His voice trailed off as Sarah disappeared behind the closed door.

Sarah's trembling fingers worked to open the envelope. Rocking in her chair by the window, she pulled out the letter and began reading. The carefully scripted words of her Aunt Emmy told a story of family illness. Sarah was devastated.

When she heard the latch on the door, she looked up to see Michael. "It's Mama." Tears gathered and trickled down her face. "Aunt Emmy writes that Mama is failing. Michael, do you think I could go home to see her?"

The following morning, Sarah and Catherine, now the eldest daughter at home, stood waiting for the stagecoach in front of the Springville Hotel. Michael had brought them to town and was now off getting supplies. Eleven-year-old, Lavina, tagged along, as she had insisted on coming too. She was to be the woman of the house until Sarah returned. All the way into town, she had pestered her mother with questions.

Long before they could see the stagecoach approaching, mother and daughter heard the bell announcing its pending arrival. Four chargers smartly decked out with handsome leather harnesses came into sight from the west. They were hitched to a fancy coach that could carry up to six passengers. The driver drew to a dusty halt in front of them and, while the horses drained a bucket of fresh water, the two women climbed aboard.

(Courtesy Stagecoach_Sovereign_Hilbandwl.jpg)

A passenger, a gentleman dressed in comfortable traveling clothes, was already onboard, his head buried in a newspaper. Though anxious to arrive in time to see their mother and grandmother, the two women were equally excited about the trip itself.

"Mama, I've never been on a stagecoach before." Catherine whispered. "I don't know whether to be excited or scared." Sarah didn't even look up as she settled herself into her seat and straightened her dress. "I know how you feel, dear."

From the seat across, a quiet friendly voice offered an answer before Sarah could say anything else. "I doubt you will want to do it again anytime soon." The man lowered the paper and smiled at his new traveling companions. With that, the carriage jolted to a start and refreshed horses led the coach into a memorable adventure.

As the stage continued east on Springville's busy Main Street, Sarah watched Catherine search for her father. As soon he had unloaded the women's carrying cases from the wagon, he had headed for the blacksmith's shop. Now, spying him, Catherine called and waved, happy to see her father acknowledge her with a nod and a smile.

Leaving the village, the coach headed east on the road leading toward China (present day Arcade) much of it within sight of the Cattaraugus Creek. From there it would head for the rolling land of the Genessee Valley toward Moscow (present day Leicester) where they would stay overnight. In Geneseo, they would transfer to another line for another long ride. With any luck they expected to arrive in Herkimer by the end of the third day. It would prove to be a long and weary trip.

As the driver picked his way along the rough surface, sometimes through wet spots near the creek, sometimes riding higher on the hills, the two women grew quiet.

"Pardon my intrusion, Ma'am." Their traveling companion addressed Sarah. He had a sincere face and was well-dressed, causing mother and daughter to be quite comfortable in spite of what could be considered audacity. "My name is Hiram Briggs. May I be so bold as to engage you in some pleasant conversation to pass the time? I pass this way with some regularity and would enjoy the company, if I may be so bold."

Sarah was aware this was a great adventure for her daughter. She knew, right away, her daughter would never forgive her if she refused to partake in some innocent pleasantries.

"Why, that would be very nice, Mr. ...Briggs, did you say?"

"Yes, Hiram Briggs. I am a teacher of Natural Science at the Springville Academy."

"Then I have no doubt there will be much we might learn from you as we proceed." Sarah smiled as Catherine nearly cut her off in her haste to be so engaged.

"What is it that causes you to travel so much, Mr. Briggs?"

Sarah's eyes widened and she turned and stared at her daughter. "Catherine, you shouldn't . . ."

"No, no, my dear woman. You mustn't be upset. We are on a rather long and wearisome trip. The question truly deserves an answer. Much as I enjoy the surroundings of Springville, my family lives in Geneva, and I frequently travel back during school recesses."

As the horses rounded a bend, a front wheel dropped into a sizeable hole catching the coach's occupants off guard. Too late, Sarah raised her arm to rescue Catherine. At the same time she grabbed the sturdy framework of the door with her other hand. Poor Catherine though had been leaning forward to listen to Mr. Brigg's story. She was caught totally off guard and lurched into the strong arms of their surprised fellow passenger. Fortunately, Mr. Briggs, not unaccustomed to these jarring

117

events, had braced his feet for what might occur. However, a young lady landing in his arms was entirely unforeseen.

*  *  *

"Both, needless to say, were quite embarrassed," Arthur commented.

"Poor Catherine." As she spoke, Rosie looked over at Jessie, but Jessie appeared to be lost in thought. "Hello, Jessie. Are you in there?" Rosie leaned forward and looked her friend in the eye. "There's a far-away look in your eyes. What are you thinking about?"

"Huh? Oh, sorry." Jessie shook her head and looked at her friend. "I was just thinking about how much the world has changed since that time. You know, like a horse and wagon was their form of transportation. Ours is a car that can travel 100 mph. (Well, it's a VW; maybe not a hundred.) Sarah and Catherine reserved seats on a stagecoach. We would take a train or a flight on an airline. Their version of 'survival' was entirely different from 'survival' in today's terms. Oh, never mind."

Looking around as if Arthur was standing somewhere nearby, she said, " I'm sorry, Arthur. What were you saying?"

Arthur just laughed and the windows rattled. "Sure is different now, isn't it Jessie?" Then he dove back into his story.

*  *  *

At a brief stop in China, a second young man joined the list of passengers while mother and daughter stretched their legs. Then all continued, leaving the familiar creek behind as they entered into the broad and gentle slopes of the Genesee Valley. While Sarah busied herself with a tricky portion of a sweater she was knitting, the lush farmland passed by at a constant pace and lulled Catherine into a restless sleep.

Late in the day, after too many hours of dirty roads, the weary group pulled to a stop at the National Exchange, a busy inn and tavern in the tiny community of Moscow. A warm meal and a fresh bed greeted the ladies, who soon retired in order to avoid the roughshod mix of men assembled in the barroom.

Early the next morning, Sarah peeked out of her window to see what the day might bring. Two men appeared to be in a quiet conversation while their heads moved to the left and right as if watching for someone or something. The men shook hands and, while one returned to the inn, the other, their driver, slipped into the barn where a fresh pair of horses neighed.

Sarah continued to watch, her curiosity piqued. A moment later the driver re-appeared, now accompanied by a young black boy carrying a cloth sack. The boy held back in the shadows of the doorway as if frozen to the ground while the driver moved directly to the back of the stagecoach. Lifting the canvas that covered a container for passenger luggage, he looked back at the boy and motioned

119

for him to come forward. Sarah read his lips as he hissed, "Quickly!" Then the boy disappeared under the canvas tarp. The driver leaned into the compartment for a moment, then climbing aboard in the driver's seat, he made his way to the front of the building.

Sarah had heard about the Underground Railroad and, while never voicing her opinion, fully supported the effort. Now it was happening in front of her. She had no reason to reach any other conclusion. A piece of her was thrilled to be involved, but that didn't minimize her worry. This meant that the stage they occupied would be a target for trouble. She decided it would be best to keep knowledge of this activity to herself as she entered the coach aware of the stowaway onboard.

The stagecoach had been well on its way toward the village of Geneseo when two roughshod men on horseback appeared from behind. The passengers watched as they approached, one on each side. Uneasy, each male passenger reached into some concealed spot and fingered an unknown item, one inside his coat, the other somewhere near his boot.

Unaware of any danger, Catherine sat at the edge of her seat peering out at the riders. "Catherine, sit back. Never you mind what's going on out there." Sarah's eyes darted from one side to the other, watching the two riders. A chill ran through her as she heard one of the men speak.

"Hold up now, driver. We need ta be talkin' with ya."

The driver snapped the reigns, urging his horses to keep up their pace. "Off with you. I got a schedule ta keep an' these passengers don't want no trouble."

"We got wind o' a run-away back there at the National. Know anythin' 'bout it?"

"Nope. Now, leave us be."

The two riders slowed their pace just a bit and, coming alongside the coach, they each took a long hard look at the passengers. The ladies sat with their heads down, Catherine seeming to read the page of a book and Sarah's hands busy with her knitting.

One hand on the framed window opening, Mr. Briggs looked out at the rider who appeared to be the leader. He was about to speak when the second rider, keeping pace on the opposite side, drew his gun. In a threatening tone he announced, "Wouldn't be reachin' fer that gun, if I was you." The barrel of his own pistol was now inches from the face of the man next to Mr. Briggs. The young man eased himself back into the seat. "Just scratching an itch." A smile crossed his face but his eyes, Sarah noted, told a different story.

Suddenly the leader kicked his horse and moved up next to the stagecoach horses. Grabbing hold of the harness, he pulled them to a stop – horses, driver, passengers and all. The furious driver spit and sputtered, but there was nothing he could do.

"We just gonna have a look 'round," the leader shouted back over his shoulder. "Jimmy, keep an eye on our driver here while I unload these passengers." Then he trotted back to the cabin and waved his gun to indicate that everyone should exit the coach. That accomplished, he dismounted.

As Catherine stepped out of the coach, Jimmy spotted her and left the driver to get a closer look at the young lady. She stood perfectly still, straight and tall, as he drew up beside her.

"Well, look what we have here," he murmured. A sly smile slid across his lips as he reached down to lift her long silky hair. Sarah could see the anger in her daughter's eyes. She held her breath, hoping her daughter would be sensible. Catherine shifted. Then, with the full force of building anger, she lifted her elbow and rammed it squarely into the ribs of the horse standing next to her.

As the surprised animal let out a loud snort, Catherine stepped away to avoid what would come next. The horse rose high on its rear legs, its forefeet pawing the air. The surprised rider slid from his saddle and tumbled to the ground, nearly breaking his neck. On his feet in a flash and ready to make the smart-alecky girl pay for her actions, he came face to face with a small black derringer. "One move toward that brave young lady and you're a dead man," Mr. Briggs threatened.

Distracted from his searching, the leader sauntered over to his sidekick. "Serves ya right, ya sick bastard. We's here ta find a run-away. Now pick up yer hat an' leave the lady alone." At that, he turned his attention back to the stagecoach and lifted the canvas off the luggage space.

Sarah held her breath as he rummaged through a number of boxes and suitcases. She wondered if anyone other than she and the driver knew who was hiding inside and let out a slight gasp when the man cursed. Hearing it, he turned and looked directly into Sarah's eyes. His were hateful piercing eyes that made Sarah want to shrink.

"Seems maybe you know somethin' you oughta be tellin' me about, Ma'am." The man continued to glare at her as he came face to face in front of her. Though she was nearly ready to faint, Sarah held his stare. In a low and clear voice, she replied, "Sir, I am merely distressed by the audacity of this interruption. My daughter and I are on our way to the bedside of my dying mother. This delay and the uncouth behavior of your companion are highly distressing. Please leave us alone so our driver can get underway again."

The slave catcher stood for a moment as if considering what to do next. Sarah nearly wilted under his cold stare, but she stood her ground. After a veritable eternity, the man walked to his horse, climbed into the saddle, and rode off, leaving his partner to scramble catching up to him.

At their Geneseo switching point, Sarah watched as driver, team and stagecoach disappeared into the shadows of a nearby barn. No one was nearby when the driver reappeared and walked by her on his way for food and drink.

"I know what you did," Sarah spoke in a low voice. "You should be proud. You are doing a good thing."

Surprised, the driver stopped without looking at her.

"Just one question," she went on. "How did they not find him?"

Still looking far into the distance, the driver responded, ". . . secret compartment for one. I'll be movin' on now, Ma'am. Thank you."

Sarah never forgot that clandestine exchange.

# New Trees

"Back here, eleven-year-old Lavina was having the time of her life," Arthur told his new friends. "Until Sarah returned she was the queen of her mother's kitchen. She strutted around in her mother's apron and, to her brothers' delight, scolded them when they teased her, and they teased her as often as possible.

Jessie raised an eyebrow and looked up from her note-taking. "Seems a bit young, don't you think?"

"Well, maybe, but back in the nineteenth century, these country girls had to get serious about life pretty early. This was only temporary, so it was good training. A girl her age might be expected to carry out any number of daily tasks – feeding the chickens, gathering eggs, churning the milk for butter, watching the little ones."

"So, in this case," Rosie chimed in, "she just took over all the meal preparation?"

"Yup. She was the only woman in the house and she was determined to take on the role of feeding her Pa and her brothers. As I recall, it was all pretty basic, but the men-folk didn't complain."

"How long was Sarah gone?"

"Seems to me, it was close to a month. Sarah's mother died just a few days after she arrived. What with the wake, the funeral and all that happens to a family at a time like that, Sarah and Catherine didn't get back until sometime in late May."

"Riding in the wagon on the way back to the farm, Michael told her about a deal he had just made to buy some new property. He was pretty excited about it. Seems he picked up several acres of new land and was going to plant a big apple orchard. He and the neighbor sat right here when they made the deal."

*       *       *

"Been thinkin', Fred. I want ta plant me an apple orchard."

Fred leaned back with a slight smile on his face and waited for what was to come.

"Ain't none around here. Seems like there might be a place or two I could sell the apples." Michael searched his neighbor's face.

Old Fred, dressed in overalls, a denim shirt and a beat-up hat that looked like it had been run over by a herd of cattle, nodded and smiled. "Gotta give ya credit,

Michael. You been here, what – maybe five years or so. Got yourself a mighty good lookin' farm. Seems to be working out pretty good for you and the Mrs.

"Well, could be better. Lost a heifer ta that cougar a year or so ago, but, all in all, me 'nd the wife, we doin' okay. Got a lot o' mouths ta feed, though, so I gotta be thinkin' all the time."

The door swung open and two boys raced into the house. It slammed shut with a loud thud while the older one tackled the little one who screamed with delight. Interrupted by the commotion, the men stopped talking and watched without interrupting the fun. Fred couldn't help shaking his head.

"Is that little nipper the baby Sarah had after you moved in?"

Michael sat back and sighed, "Yup. He's a real pistol, that boy. Keeps up real good with his older brothers, he does."

"My goodness sake. How he has grown."

At that, Michael put a stop to the boys' activities. "Jacob. Herman. That'll be 'nough. Either ya quiets down, or git yerselves outa the house."

The boys looked up, then looked at each other and giggled. As they scrambled to get up off the floor, Herman was about to say something, but Jacob cut him off.

"Kin we have some maple, Pa?"

Michael rolled his eyes as he nodded. "Go find yer sister fer some sweets. – Now, git!" He looked back at Fred, shrugged his shoulders and, again, sighed.

"Sorry, Fred. Now, what was we sayin'?"

"You was tellin' me about yer new apple orchard."

"Well, boys, now, don't exactly have one yet. I was hopin' ya might consider sellin' off a few acres of yer land across the road. Ya got that big hunk of it over there, 'nd I sure could use a small piece."

Fred stood, arched his back just enough to stretch out a couple of aches and pains, and walked to the window. As he looked out at the land across the road, Michael watched and wondered what was going on in his neighbor's head. From the faraway look in the man's eyes, Michael knew it would be best to keep his trap shut and wait for his reply.

Without turning and still looking out the window, Fred finally replied.

"Well, Michael, like you said, there's a lot of land on that piece, over a hundred acres. Don't much use it right now, but been thinkin' to hand it over to my son in a few years." He stopped and remained silent for what seemed like an eternity. Michael could almost feel some kind of war going on in his neighbor's head.

Breaking the silence, Michael offered. "The piece I'm wonderin' 'bout is that hilly land right next ta the road. Pretty steep fer plantin' or fer cow pasture. Not near as good as the piece right above it. I can see why Lawrence might be wantin' that piece, but –"

"Michael, my friend," Fred turned back, nodded his head, and looked his neighbor in the eye. He spoke so low Michael could barely hear him. ". . . you 'nd Sarah been

128

mighty good neighbors. Always willing to lend a hand when the need come. Ya got a good workin' farm here, and I can see what yer planning'. I'll be happy ta work out a deal. Let's you 'nd me figure out a fair price fer what ya need."

Two weeks later, Michael stood at the edge of the road with his three oldest boys. They were all looking at a seven acre patch of hillside they now owned. A few large oak and maple trees were scattered among a large quantity of scrub brush. It would all have to be cut down to make room for the new fruit trees.

"Well, boys, these trees ain't gonna come down by themselves. Let's git started." As Michael and Simon began working out a plan for taking down the first tree, a tall old maple, Conrad and George started slashing away all the low brush.

Morning after morning, the men headed over to the new patch of land as soon as the cows had been milked. All three of the boys were old enough to hold their own and Michael was enjoying their company. While they worked, they bantered and sassed, and, sometimes even weighed in on more serious conversations.

"Hey, Pa. You heard anything about this guy, Lincoln?" Simon and his brothers knew their pa couldn't read or write very well, but they also knew he was no dummy. Whenever he went to town or to the mill, Michael kept his ears tuned in to the topic of the day. The latest talk these days was about a young ex-congressman from Illinois by the name of Abraham Lincoln.

Michael was half way through a swing of his ax as Simon opened the conversation. The ax landed and wedged deep in the growing notch.

"Heard a couple of men talkin' 'bout him at the mill the other day." He jerked the ax out and took another swing. "Seems he's getting' inta a big debate over slavin' in the South. You mark my word, ain't heard the last of him, we ain't."

"What do you think's gonna happen, Pa? Everybody's getting pretty steamed up over whether the new states should allow slavery."

Don't know the answer ta that, Boy. Just know, if we sees a runaway 'round here, well, I be the first ta help 'em. Ain't *nobody* got no right ta use 'em as slaves."

Michael took one more powerful swing at the tree and stood back to watch it come crashing to the ground. Before any of them could begin clearing the limbs away, the clang of a bell filtered its way up the hillside.

"'Enough said 'bout that, now. Best we keep our thoughts ta ourselves 'bout the runaways. Some of them slave catchers get wind o' what I said, they be pushin' their way inta the house ta see if we hidin' somebody. – Now, that's yer Ma callin' us fer dinner. Don't want ta keep her waitin' long."

Later, as the family finished up the last of the pork stew Sarah had prepared, Sarah and Catherine retold their experience with the runaway on their stagecoach. Jacob, who had heard the entire story already, busied himself gathering and munching on the few remaining crumbs from two loaves of corn bread Sarah had served with the meal.

"Do ya think we'll ever be hidin' somebody here, Pa?" Lavina asked.

"Well, ain't seen none around here yet, and they been runnin' for years. Most likely, not."

In the end, though, everyone in the family knew what they should do if an escaped slave ever came around.

\*       \*       \*

"You know, it never crossed my mind that we're talking about the years leading up to the Civil War," Rosie said. She frowned and looked away to the far corner of the room as if she felt the weight of the issues on her own shoulder. "I don't know what I would have done if someone like that asked me for help."

Arthur offered a partial response.

"Michael probably wouldn't have known about this, but years later I heard someone talk about a house over in Riceville that was part of the Underground Railroad. A fellow by the name of Joseph Remington and his wife, Amanda, were involved in an alternate route to Canada. Nobody really knows how many people they actually helped, but they were ready. They would feed the runaway and let them rest a bit. Later they would hide them in a hay wagon and ride to the next destination ten or twelve miles to the north.

131

# Curds and Whey

Sarah blew out the candle and slipped into bed. "Michael . . ." Though it wasn't planned that way, the word came out in almost a whisper. Sarah wasn't sure how well this news would be received.

"Michael!"

Her only response was the pitch black silence of the room she shared with her husband. Then she heard it, the sighing-like noise that told her Michael was already out for the night.

"MICHAEL!"

"A . . . What? . . . What'd ya say?" Michael raised his head and took note of the shadow of his wife. He didn't need to see her face . . . was glad he couldn't see it . . . because he knew, at that moment, she was not particularly happy. Not that he, himself, was exactly thrilled to be awakened.

"What ya needin', Woman? Can't a man get some sleep?"

"I am with child . . . AGAIN."

The silence returned as Michael tried to comprehend what had just been said. Finally . . ."Yer, WHAT?"

"We're going to have another baby."

"Now, what's ya go 'nd do a thing like that fer?" "Me? . . . It takes two, you know." Sarah nudged her lunatic husband as he sat up, suddenly fully conscious of what had just come out of his mouth.

"I thought we was done with all that . . . what with yer gittin' older . . . and stuff."

Sarah gave him a shove that sent him flat on the bed. "Old, my FOOT!" ...hard enough to fully bring him to his senses.

Michael looked perplexed. "Well, this is a fine howdy do. Keep this up 'nd we be runnin' outta names."

Silence returned to the bedroom while both let the real meaning of what Sarah had just announced set in. Sarah waited . . . waited for what she knew would eventually be said by her husband.

"Well, Woman, God gave us another child. Least we kin do is give it a good home 'nd keep it safe. We'll make do. – Now, I'm gonna get me some sleep. Mornin' comes early this time of year." After a moment's hesitation, he lifted his head and mumbled to no one in particular. "Needs all the sleep I can git ta keep up with this family."

As she settled in, Sarah thought how much she loved this man. Long ago she had accepted his strange ways of showing his love for her. She fell asleep smiling.

A few short hours later, the sun once again found its way over the crest of the hill facing the house. Charlie, the family's Rhode Island Red rooster, raised his head, ruffled his feathers, and strutted over to the same fencepost he stood on every morning for his daily announcement. Perched on the post, he raised his head, stuck out his neck and let go with his famous call.

Sleepy heads were lifted off of cozy, warm feather pillows as every person in the house responded to the call. Some leaped out of bed. Some dragged themselves out from under the blanket. Some rolled over and tried to ignore the testy noise. Within mere minutes, though, the house was alive and a new day had sprung.

It was a fine summer morning. The sun suggested it would be another hot day. With the nighttime chill still in the air, Michael and the boys took on the task of feeding the animals and milking the cows. Though the routine rarely changed, Michael announced the plan for today's milk.

"George, soon as we done here, you and Conrad gather up the milk we took last night along with this mornin's milkin'. Cart it over ta the Franktown Cheese Factory. With what we git today, we should have us near 50 pounds of product for 'em."

George hitched up the horses while Conrad pulled several buckets of the previous day's milk out of the spring-fed vat that kept it cool from the summer heat. With the combined load complete, George and Conrad climbed aboard.

"Git up, Babe."

"Gonna be a scorcher today, Conrad."

"Yup. Maybe Pa will let us go swimming down at the Connoisarauley Creek this afternoon."

"Yea. Well, let's just get this milk processed, then see what Pa has in mind for the day."

As the boys pulled up to the cheese factory, a man appeared at the door.

"Mornin' Mr. Smith."

"Mornin', boys. How much you got for me today?"

George turned and looked back at the load. "I'd say near fifty pounds, or so."

That'd be good enough. Bring 'em over and let's get 'em weighed in."

While George and Mr. Smith hauled the milk to the scales, Conrad kept his eyes on the operation. Though a small factory, the process and the men who worked there were always interesting to watch. Milk brought in by area farmers was soon transferred to a large vat and heated up to just a few degrees warmer than cold. That part puzzled Conrad.

"What does that mean – a few degrees warmer than cold?"

"Believe it or not, Conrad, we check the milk by putting our elbow in it," one of the workers told him. He rolled up his shirt sleeve and pointed to an encrusted elbow that looked like it hadn't seen soap and water in a month. "Milk's good when it feels good on the elbow."

Conrad stared at the exposed body part and shook his head in disbelief.

"Then what?" He was beginning to get grossed out.

"Then we add a piece of rennit."

"What's rennit?"

"It's some stuff that breaks down the milk; comes from the inners of a young cow and makes the milk curdle. When the milk is all nice 'nd thick, we draw off the curds and pack 'em in a drainer. Then we put 'em in a press for twenty-four hours."

Conrad decided he might never eat cheese again. When the worker saw the disgusted look on Conrad's face, he laughed and changed the subject. "You be interested in taking home some whey? We got some ready for the takin'."

George and Mr. Smith had joined the others just in time to hear this offer. Without hesitating, George piped up, "Be glad to take it off your hands. Pa's done that before. Good food for the pigs." He turned to Mr. Smith. "Seems a good trade for the milk instead of you payin' us today."

With a broad smile, the factory owner nodded in agreement.

A half hour later the boys pulled up in front of their pa. "Got some whey for the pigs, Pa."

"Good. Take it on down, Boy. Ain't fed-um yet."

Along about mid-morning Little Bear appeared out of nowhere. Coming around the corner of the shed, he greeted Michael and the boys. Though he had probably been walking since early morning, he didn't look the least bit tired. The young Native American man was dressed in deerskin trousers and moccasins and, unlike their previous encounter, wore no shirt. A straight black line of hair not more than an inch wide ran from his forehead to the nap of his neck. A long thin knife lay in a deerskin sheath tied with a cord around his waist. He was a sight to behold, and the boys each took an uneasy step backward at his sudden appearance.

"Howdy, Little Bear." Michael turned and offered his hand in greeting. "Been 'xpectin' you. See ya got my message. We be needin' ta build a new pen fer the pigs. Used ta keep just three or four, but now we gots nine of 'em. Sure can use your help."

Little Bear looked at the outstretched hand and just nodded. "Where will you build the pen?"

Though unaccustomed to the ways of these people whose land was now his, Michael realized that a long conversation was just not going to happen. He led Little Bear to a spot where he had been building up a pile of lumber over the last couple of months. After pacing off a rough outline where he thought the pen might be built, he checked to see if Little Bear understood.

Little Bear stood, feet planted on the ground, his arms crossed at his chest. To the boys, he looked like he was about to give the order for dozens of his friends to come swooping down on the white man's house.

137

Instead, he just asked to use Michael's tools. "I run too far to bring my own tools," he stated when he saw the boys give him a curious look."

At this point, George, who was fascinated by this exchange, jumped into the conversation. "I'll get the tools, Pa, 'nd I'll stay here with Little Bear to help him." He turned and looked at the young man. "That is, if Little Bear is okay with that."

Michael searched the visitor's face, but could detect no unwillingness on his part. "That'd be a good idea, Boy. You two work on the pen. The rest of us kin git on with the farm work."

Over the next several days, Little Bear and George worked together and became best of friends.

# Hayin' Time

"By 1860, Michael and Sarah were actually doing quite well," Arthur reported. "On a day-to-day basis, the tension over slaves between the North and the South didn't leave much of a mark on this area. Farmers were too busy making a living off the land. Meanwhile, here, the family's twelfth child had been born, a tiny package of a girl named Louisa. Michael had added a sizable barn to his collection of buildings, and his animals were doing a fine job of supporting the growing family."

"So, how many animals did the family have," Jessie quizzed.

As Arthur thought, Jessie and Rosie felt the now familiar breath of air moving about the room.

"Ah, yes. As I recall, there were 12 cows, 5 horses, a mule and 2 oxen. Michael always favored using the oxen, but the 'girls' were getting pretty old. More and more, he had to rely on his draft horses to get the work done.

"What about the pigs?" Rosie asked.

"The pigs . . . of course! He generally kept about 6 or 7 pigs. Oh, and I almost forgot. There was also their dog, Spike, and three cats that lived out in the barn. . . . kept the rodent population down to a reasonable number that way.

"All in all, though, 1860 was a NOT a good year for the family."

*        *        *

It was a hot summer that year, but thanks to a few intermittent rain storms, the fields were producing record level crops. By July, Michael realized the first cutting of hay had become the highest priority. The back breaking task of scything began as Michael, Simon, George and Conrad worked their way across acre after acre of green covered earth. With one eye always watching out for a rainstorm that could endanger them, or at least interrupt their work, Michael led his crew in their toils.

"We got ourselves a good crop o' hay this year, Sarah." Michael felt pretty good about their life as he brought his wife up to date after the evening meal.

Sarah walked over to where her husband was sitting. She wrapped her arms around him and gave him a peck on his leathery neck. "You've done well, Husband. Could you have ever imagined this when we talked about moving to this area thirteen years ago? Life was so different in Herkimer."

Sarah began to knead her husband's tired shoulders. Her strong thumbs dug into muscles that ached from hours of swinging the heavy scythe back and forth, and Michael groaned as she worked. With his eyes closed, he leaned back into the hands that had shared his ups and downs, supported him and always demonstrated her love for him over the years.

"The upper field is all cut. If it don't rain tomorrow, we be loadin' it up 'nd stowin' it in the barn the day after."

"You should let the boys do more of that kind of work, Michael. There's three of them and they're old enough to carry on that work pretty much on their own."

"Now, Sarah," Michael always hated it when Sarah started making suggestions like that. "ya knows I can't just turn over everythin' ta them. I'll be goldarned if I'll sit around 'nd just watch."

This banter between husband and wife was not uncommon. Over twenty-five years, their lives, their children, their recent success on this farm, all wove together into a loving bond sealed by the support of their twelve children.

The rain, in fact, did stay away the next day, and on the following morning Michael hitched up the horses to a freshly greased hay wagon and began the tedious task of moving the hay to his new barn where it could dry and cure. Eventually the barn would be filled with enough hay to supply his cattle and horses through the long winter.

The boys had raked the newly cut hay into furrows just far enough apart to allow the wagon to pass between them. Michael guided the team between rows while the boys pitched the fresh hay onboard. Simon, standing on the moving surface, received the hay from alternate sides and expertly stowed it against a seven-foot-high back brace, constantly moving forward toward a matching brace at the front until the entire wagon was full.

*(By permission of the Project Avalon Forum)*

Load after load, hour after hour, the men labored under the hot July sun. Every so often, Martha or William would show up, traipsing across the field with a big jug of ice tea, a welcome and refreshing break from the difficult task at hand.

The supper hour had arrived and fled away, and the field was not fully cleared. Michael was determined to finish the job before quitting for the night. The men had just emptied a wagon into the barn, and everyone was dog tired and ready to quit. Knowing this, Michael hesitated before speaking, but was able to find one small shred of energy left in his own body.

"Come on, boys. Just one more load 'nd we done."

A collective groan was their only reply as Michael snapped the reins.

"Tek, tek, git-up, now." Off they went, dragging themselves up the hill for one final load.

Nearly an hour passed before the field was clear and the wagon loaded to the brim. Michael sat atop the mound of hay, reins in both hands, guiding his team toward the rutted lane that led back down the hill. Simon and George climbed aboard and hung on to the framework at the rear of the wagon. Conrad, though just as tired, decided to walk and kept pace off to one side. As the team passed between two posts that marked the entrance to the lane, they surprised a rattle snake coiled up next to one of the posts. The snake raised its head and announced its presence with the familiar rattle of its tail.

Only a short distance from the ill-tempered snake, one of the horses let out a loud 'whinny' and tried to rear up on its hind legs. The other, confused by its partner's actions, shied away. Without warning, the horses began to run and Michael was thrown from his position atop the load. He pitched, head first, toward the ground and was stopped only by the harness tongue that both separated and connected the two horses.

Conrad was the only one of the three who actually saw what took place. He watched in horror while his father fell into the rigging. He watched the second horse raise his right foreleg and land a kick squarely into his father's shoulder. He watched his father fall to the ground as the wagon moved forward and passed over him.

The frenzied horses made a wild dash down the hill, hay flying off the wagon all the way down. Simon was thrown off when one of the wheels careened off a rock jutting out of the ground. George, who managed to stay on the wagon, made a vain attempt to reach the front, hoping he could somehow re-establish control of the team.

Back at the gate, Michael lay face down in the grass-covered center of the lane. The rattler slithered its way toward him.

"Pa! – PA, get up!" Conrad ran to his father waving his arms to scare off the menacing snake.

Out of nowhere, George appeared holding a thick rock the size of a dinner plate high above his head. With a loud, "Ah-h-h!" the rock came crashing down on the wayward snake.

". . . And, just in the nick of time." Conrad smirked and cocked his head as he looked back at his brother. Not just the day's sweat, but more likely, the product of this awful accident poured from his face, neck and arms. One quick look at their unconscious father confirmed they were now dealing with a serious situation. The ground under Michael's shoulder appeared tainted with the color red.

Michael let out a low moan as he regained his senses and the boys gingerly rolled him over. Opening his eyes, he looked around. "What? . . . What happened?" His eyes met the eyes of his sons. Then he again lost consciousness.

George took a hard look at his father's wounds, then turned to his brother and shook his head. "Looks like we better find Dr. Wilson. You ride to get the doc. I'll bring Pa to the house."

With the strength of biblical Samson, he picked up his father and carried him in his arms down the length of the hill.

All the commotion from the horses when they dashed down the hill brought Sarah and the other children out the door. They watched in horror, knowing that Simon tried in vain to reach the front or the reins of the wagon, but still hung onto the wagon. When the horses came to a stop of their own accord in front of the barn, Sarah's attention was drawn back to the lane and the hill. She screamed as George came into view, the limp body of her husband in his arms.

When he reached the road in front of the house, she got a firsthand look at the outcome of whatever had occurred at the top of the hill. Michael's bloodied shoulder and his caved-in chest were sufficient evidence of the seriousness of the situation.

"Take him to the house, George. Lay him on our bed."

Then, turning to speak to Conrad, she realized he was already on his way to the barn. She called to tell him to get the doctor, but he was already saddling one of the other horses.

Supper was never served that evening. From time to time, one or two might sample a ladle full of beef stew growing cold on the stove. Sarah never left her husband's side. Rather, concerned children maintained a constant path to and from the bed and the stove as they brought warm wash clothes to clean his wounds – and everyone waited for Dr. Wilson.

# Overcast

Sarah sat in her rocking chair staring out into the darkness. When the good doctor had arrived, she again heard what had occurred up on the hill. Now, while he examined Michael's injuries, there was nothing she could do. So she retreated to her sacred spot, her rocker, and waited in silence while the doctor examined Michael. The children somehow knew their mother needed to be alone.

After what seemed a lifetime, the doctor withdrew from the bedroom. Closing the door behind him, he raised one finger to his lips for the benefit of those who were waiting in the parlor.

"Sh-h-h . . . Your father is asleep. Where is your mother?"

One of the children motioned toward the door leading to the family's primary gathering space. Nodding, he turned and left the parlor in search of Sarah.

147

Teary eyed, Sarah looked up. "How bad is it, Doctor?"

"Well, Sarah, I can't lie to you. Michael took a terrible tumble. It appears he broke at least two ribs. In due time they will heal, but I'm more concerned about the damage from the horse's kick."

"But, he'll survive, won't he?"

"Y-y-yes, he can survive the blow to his shoulder IF he can avoid an infection."

Sarah turned her head away, gazed out the window and sighed.

"I must tell you, Sarah, if your husband's shoulder becomes infected . . . well."

"Dr. Wilson?"

A voice from behind the doctor interrupted their discussion and he turned to see the children huddled in a small group off to the side. George and Conrad were standing at the back. Catherine was holding Jacob. Simon stood with his hands on the shoulders of eight-year-old Herman. William and Lovina huddled together in their midst. Only baby Louisa was missing, at peace as she slept in her cradle.

There was an emptiness in the children's eyes that told of their sadness, but the doctor noted something more. The boys stood straight as rods, their jaws set. The girls watched Catherine as she spoke and tried to mirror her look of determination.

Catherine, her muscles tight, began trembling as she again spoke.

"Doctor Wilson?"

"Yes, Catherine"

"What can we do?"

"Well, your father's condition is dangerous." He turned and looked at Sarah before going on. Then, turning back to the children, he continued, "Your mother is a strong, capable woman. She will probably be spending most of her time for the next few weeks tending to your father."

The doctor took a step closer to the children. He looked from one to another to another knowing he had their full attention. "You girls – you will need to tend to the cooking and the care of the house. The less your mother has to think about, the more energy she'll have to see to your father's welfare without becoming sick herself. Boys, as far as I'm concerned, your Pa's done for the season. I don't want to see him working this farm for at least three months. You boys know what to do. Go out and make it happen."

As he spoke, he looked at their solemn faces and could tell that every one of them, from oldest to youngest, understood the situation. "Now, I suggest that all of you get some sleep while I finish up here with your mother. Tomorrow is a new day. It will be your day to show your parents what you can do."

At that, he turned back to Sarah. A river of tears was running down her face as she watched the doctor and her brood. "They'll do ya proud, Sarah. You watch."

"Oh, I know they will, Doctor. I know they will."

149

As the children disappeared into their rooms, he gave Sarah some final instructions before making one last check on Michael's condition. At least, for the moment, Michael was lying still and quiet. So he bid farewell and returned to his own home and bed.

With the arrival of dawn, Charlie the rooster, strutted from his coop, flew up to his post, and announced another day. Without a word spoken, the three oldest boys arose, dressed and headed for the barn. Though George and Conrad knew exactly what needed to be done, they deferred to Simon when he laid out the morning's plans. He was the oldest. He would be in charge. That, they knew, was the way Pa would want it.

Meanwhile, Catherine began preparing breakfast for the family. Surrounded by well-intentioned younger siblings willing to do their part, she could hardly think.

"What can I do, Cathy?"

Where are the plates?"

How much milk goes in the pitcher?"

Nearly overwhelmed by her sisters' unusual interest, she soon lost her cheerful smile and began muttering something about being alone. One by one, the others took leave of the kitchen area and found other things to busy themselves.

Sarah was nowhere to be seen. Behind the closed bedroom door she remained by Michael's side and saw to his every need. The wounds must be cleaned. New patches would surely keep the fever at bay. She must, above all, find ways to distract her husband and keep his mind off the farm's many needs.

. . . and the first day passed without mishap.

Day two: The red sky of the morning horizon suggested the area might expect less than pleasant weather. The boys had finished morning chores. The girls had, after sending a wholesome breakfast to the bedroom for Michael and Sarah, equally satisfied their starving brothers.

As George and Conrad stood under the broad limbs of a maple tree not far from the house, the breeze shifted and leaves on the tree turned themselves around. Conrad broke the silence.

"Rain's coming."

"Yup."

"What about Pa?"

"What about him?"

"Do you think we can keep him out of the barn when he starts feeling better?"

George scratched his head and looked out across the span of property their parents had developed. "Can't say as I think so. You know how he is. His heart and soul are in this land."

"Yes, but you heard the doc. He sounded pretty serious when he said Pa shouldn't be working the farm for a while."

Thunder rolled through the distant hills, and to the west the sky grew dark. Uncomfortable with the conversation about their ailing father, George found reason to change the subject.

"Looks like we're not gonna get anything done in the fields today."

The conversation came to a standstill as a bolt of lightning streaked across the western sky. At the count of 'ten' a grumble of thunder bounced its way to their ears, announcing the current location of a storm not far away.

"Two miles".

The words came out of their mouths almost in unison, and they looked at each other and laughed.

"Remember when Pa taught us how to figure out the distance of a storm?"

"Yea. The next one should tell us how much time we have before we're in the middle of it."

Again, the western sky sent a shaft of light from somewhere above to somewhere on Earth. Again the boys counted and, this time, the magic number was seven.

"Movin' this way pretty fast," Conrad offered. "Better bring the horses in before the lightning gets too close." Off they went, running at an easy pace toward the pasture at the edge of the barn.

Within minutes the horses were safely in their stalls. The boys stood in the barn and heard the rain begin. A light sprinkle expanded into a steady rain that rattled on the roof and ran off its edges, splashing on the ground twenty feet below. A crack of lightning lit up the hillside across the road, splitting the air with a noise that would raise the dead.

Not ten seconds later another charge of lightning ripped through the sky as the rain now drove against every available surface.

As fast as the summer storm arrived over the hills, it also left. The rumbling and grumbling of thunder could still be heard as it moved away. Now, though, the sound came from the opposite direction and weakened as it moved east. On the farm the sun returned, a scattering of white puffy clouds replaced the rain-filled sky and the air yielded the scent of summer freshness.

Conrad leaned against the barn door, his hands in his pockets, breathing in the fresh air. As he stood there, the sound of a horse clip-clopping its way down the road drew his attention.

"Hey, George. Lawrence and Lydia Frank are headed this way."

In the middle of mucking out a stable, George only grunted and continued his chore.

"Whoa, Brady. Whoa there." Lawrence pulled at the reins and nodded to Conrad as his horse brought the buggy to a standstill.

"Conrad, how goes it?"

"Just fine, Mr. Frank. . . .and you, Mrs. Frank?"

"Thank you, Conrad. I am quite well."

Lawrence got right to the point. "We're stopping by to see your father. Understand he took a mean kick the other day. Figured with the storm passing, now'd be a good time to come calling."

"Nice of you, Mr. Frank. Pa's still laid up in bed, but likely he'll be glad to see you. If you'd like to leave your buggy here, I'll get a bucket of water for Brady."

At that, Conrad helped Lydia down and the couple headed for the house.

"Come along, Brady. Let's get you some water and, maybe, a handful of oats."

July passed under the heat of the sun. Day by day Michael's wounds healed and his spirits improved with the healing.

"Michael."

Sarah stood on the porch watchful of her husband's every move as he hobbled across the front yard.

"You know what Dr. Wilson said. No work for three months."

A groan escaped from Michael's lips as he tried to lean down to pick up a dead branch, his broken ribs screaming for relief.

"Danged if I gonna sit around 'nd do nothing, Woman. I gots me a farm and there is work needs doin'"

**"Michael!"**

He stopped, turned and made a half step in her direction. His eyes flashed as he answered and the frustration in his voice said it all. "Dang you, Woman, I heard just 'bout enough o' yer pesterin'. Now, I'm gonna do what I wants ta do, and you or no doctor gonna stop me." At that, he stomped off toward the barn.

This was Michael's first visit to his beloved animals since the accident and he was too excited to care what anyone else thought or said. When he reached the barn, he tried with all his might to slide open the lower door leading to the horse stalls. The door, though, heavy and in need of fresh grease on its rollers, refused to budge.

"George! Conrad! Somebody!"

He roared for someone, anyone to help him. Once more he leaned hard against the door and pushed. A searing pain shot through his upper body as the fragile shoulder wound tore open and he collapsed to the ground.

Rushing to him from inside, the boys threw open the door. As it rolled out of the way, they found their father lying in a growing pool of blood.

"Oh, my God. What has he done now?"

The question needed no answer for Conrad. He threw a saddle on the back of a nearby horse, mounted the beast, and leaned down to speak to his brother.

"Pa's in a heap of trouble again. Get him back to the house while I go get Doc Wilson.'

Weak-kneed, Michael finally stood up. He leaned hard on George's shoulder and stumbled back to the house and his soon-to-be-angry wife. He knew he was about to receive a severe tongue-lashing, and rightfully so.

In spite of Doc Wilson's best efforts, late into the next night the fever set in. Michael lay in his bed. Beads of sweat rose on his forehead and rolled down his face and neck. The children, once again, kept a steady stream of cool basin water in front of their mother as she fought the

155

infection. Night turned into daylight, and daylight left and came again. With each coming of the day, Michael lost strength, moaned more, and began thrashing about in an effort to ward off the inevitable.

Ever vigilant, ever faithful, Sarah remained by his side. She prayed as she refreshed the cloth, dipping it into the cool water and wringing it out. She whispered soft nothings into his ear as she pressed the cool, damp cloth to his forehead. She tried to close her eyes when he slept. Though her own body was near exhaustion, she never left his side.

It was evening . . . the fourth day. Mary and Nancy had returned to their parents' side from their own homes. Nancy's two little ones kept all the siblings distracted and busy. One by one, though, when the time arrived for goodbyes, each of Michael's offspring came to his bedside, stood next to him, and found their own way of saying farewell. Everyone knew the end was near.

From oldest to youngest, the children had come and gone. Only Sarah remained. A calmness settled on the darkened room. Sarah watched as her husband ceased his restless movements; watched as he stopped his moans and groans. He opened his eyes and looked into the eyes of his wife. Dragging his arm across the surface of the bed, he laid a hand on hers. His eyes, tired and sad, never blinked and never moved away. His mouth opened, words ready to be spoken seemingly stuck somewhere inside. Finally, in something more than a whisper and less than out loud, Michael spoke.

"Sarah, I ain't said much, but ya needs ta know . . . I always loved ya."

His eyes closed, his head turned slowly to one side and his breath slid out from between closed lips.

# The Longest Day

When Arthur finished his description of Michael's deathbed, an ominous silence settled on the room. Rosie reached into her bag, pulled out a clean white tissue and dabbed her eyes so she could see how Jessie was handling the moment. Jessie, at the same time, was straightening her blouse sleeve, wiping away any evidence of dampness.

Rosie broke the silence. "Poor Sarah."

"Poor Sarah!" Jessie glared at Rosie, not because she was mad at her, but because she was, well, just mad. "If I were Sarah, I'd have been hopping mad. That man's death was all because of his own stupid arrogance. He was told not to get involved in the farm work, and he didn't listen. Sarah's the one who paid the price." She kicked at a nearby piece of firewood.

Letting the girls vent for a moment, Arthur finally spoke. "Oh, she got angry all right, but not right away. For at least a while, she was too busy and too much in shock."

158

*     *     *

The days that followed were a whirlwind of activities. Sarah moved through each day as if pushed by an invisible force that directed her from place to place and person to person. Mary, the eldest child, was designated to take charge of the household. Henry brought Nancy back from East Otto, but had to immediately return to his own farm to tend their cattle. After he left, Nancy remained by her mother's side, holding her hand and consoling her when she broke down and cried. Catherine made it her business to look after Lavina and baby Louisa. Lavina, a vulnerable fourteen-year-old, found her strength in watching over six-year old-Jacob.

Each of the girls went about her business with the same matter-of-fact calmness their mother had demonstrated all their lives. There was much to be done. Arrangements must be made for the wake and burial. The parlor must be thoroughly cleaned and furniture rearranged to make room for Michael's casket.

Simon, the oldest of the boys, took responsibility for washing and preparing his father's body. As he glanced around the room at his siblings, he mumbled something about this being a job no one should have to face. Meanwhile, George and Conrad went to work building a pine box for Michael's body. They were swift and silent in their efforts, each aware that the product of their labors would, in a way, honor the body it carried. A few trimmings were added to the exterior to enhance its appearance.

Of course, all the boys still kept up their other duties. There were cows to be milked, animals to be fed, pens and cages that must be mucked out and cleaned. Milk must still be delivered to the cheese factory and eggs taken to market.

Word traveled fast. Everyone in the area was well aware Michael had been seriously injured. They also knew he was not one to be sitting on his duff for a long time. Reactions filtered back to the family.

"Not surprised . . ."

"Poor Sarah . . ."

". . . all those kids."

"They'll get through it."

For a full day and a night, the family stood by the casket. The front door was draped in black, a sign for friends and neighbors to stop by to express condolences. No one met them at the roadside to care for each horse and carriage when they arrived. Upon crossing the threshold into the parlor, all could see that the clock on the mantle was stopped at the exact hour of Michael's death. A few flowers near the coffin offered the fresh aroma of the fields Michael had worked so hard to cultivate.

Sarah, dressed in a plain black dress with a matching bonnet, sat huddled in an armless wooden chair next to the casket, her eyes downcast except for brief moments when she acknowledged the condolences of friends. The adult daughters, too, were dressed in black.

Michael lay in his Sunday best and looked to be asleep. Jacob, Herman, William and Lovina came to Sarah's side only when outsiders were not present. The older boys, too, were often absent, finding it more to their liking to look into the needs of Michael's animals.

On the morning of the burial, overcast skies threatened to send rain to further dampen spirits. Fred Frank and his son, Lawrence, had agreed to help. Each showed up with a pair of draft horses and a wagon, one for the coffin, the other to carry Michael's offspring to the cemetery just down the road. Simon hitched a horse and carriage for Sarah, Mary and Catherine. Henry and Nancy would follow in their own buckboard.

Sarah stood for a long time facing her husband. With trembling hand, she reached out to touch him just one more time. It was as if no one else were in the room. There was just Sarah and Michael.

A gentle touch made her realize she was not alone. Two sons had come to her side, Simon on her left and George on her right.

"It's time to go, Mother."

As her boys backed her away from the casket, forever
 away from her husband, Sarah's knees began to buckle, but two young men kept her from falling. Then she turned and walked away from the only man she had ever loved.

Too soon – much too soon -- Sarah stepped down from the carriage and began the short walk to the gravesite. Mary was on her left and Catherine stood next to her on the right. Empty of all feelings, she followed her boys who carried the long narrow box to a spot where a hole had been dug. She couldn't look at the hole, couldn't think about what would soon happen. Instead she looked up at a stately elm tree, one of several scattered on the hillside. A thin ray of morning sunlight found its way through branches and rested on the casket. Men removed hats. Women bowed their heads. Someone spoke some words. The rest she couldn't remember.

# Coping

The hours after the burial turned to days, the days to weeks. Sarah spent those days carrying out the endless tasks of a busy mother. Though she ached on the inside, she remained composed and stoic for the sake of her children. In the privacy of her own bedroom, though, she couldn't cease her weeping. Each night, in the bed she had shared with Michael for so many years, she fell into a fitful slumber longing to hear his words and feel his arms around her just one more time.

As the season changed, the air cooled and the leaves on the trees turned from green to various shades of orange, red and yellow. Then, like Michael, the leaves, too, died and disappeared. Sarah awoke one crispy autumn morning in a new and different frame of mind. *He didn't have to die*, she thought. *The foolish man did it to himself. If he would just have listened to me – done what the doctor told him, he wouldn't have gotten that infection. He would still be here."* And anger replaced her overwhelming sense of emptiness.

Sarah found proper expression for these new feelings in her daily housework. With the energy of her new-found fury, she banged pots and pans and went about the house ignoring the kind expressions of love offered by her babies. She sank deeper and deeper into her inner self. Most everything in her life was either wrong or broken. She snapped at her children, found their simplest antics less than amusing, and stomped through the house maddened by the world her husband had left behind.

As six-year-old Jacob ran into the house one wet afternoon, he left a trail of mud from the doorway far into the room. Though not an unfamiliar scene in any farmhouse on a wet day, when Sarah saw what he had done, she glared at him and threw her hands into the air.

"You thoughtless little imp. Look at what you've done."

Abandoning the meal she was preparing, she reached into a cabinet, grabbed hold of a bucket and washrag and shoved them into his hands. "You will clean up that mess right now, young man, and *then* you will go to your room. There will be no supper for you."

The other children froze, staring in amazement, as they watched her unusual behavior. Never, in all their years, had their mother spoken to any of her children like this. The weeks and months since their father's death had been difficult. There was no denying their mother had her moods. But, this – this was more than they could bear.

"Mother!" Catherine's voice was sharp and caught Sarah off guard. "Mother. That's enough."

Sarah made a slow turn and stared at her grown-up daughter.

"You've got to stop what you're doing. We simply cannot stand it anymore. Somehow you have got to come back to our world. We need you, Mother. We need you."

*       *       *

Rosie and Jessie sat spellbound, not by Sarah's reaction, so much as by Catherine's critical intervention.

"What did Sarah do?" Rosie asked.

"She went to her bedroom, buried her head in her pillow and sobbed for a good thirty minutes. When she stopped, she sat on the edge of her bed and covered her face with her hands. About a minute later, Sarah sucked in a deep breath, stood up and walked over to the dresser."

"Yea?" Both Rosie and Jessie had their eyes glued on each other.

Arthur continued. "There was a small mirror there, much like the one Michael had given to Nancy before her wedding. Sarah took the mirror in her hand, and lifted it to study her face, which I must say, looked pretty pathetic at that moment. After a while she picked up her brush and began to fix her hair. It was the first time she really fixed herself up since Michael had died."

In unison, Jessie and Rosie asked, "Then?"

165

"Then she put the mirror down, left the bedroom and went out to find Jacob. When she found him, she wrapped her arms around him in a great big hug and promised him she would never, never do that again.

"That was the last day Sarah wore the black dress. She ditched her frown, too. Back from her tortuous journey through depression, she began to wave to the neighbors as they drove by on their buckboards or in their wagons. She sometimes joined one of the boys when they went to Springville for supplies."

Arthur sighed. "You can't imagine what a relief it was to see Sarah cheerful again."

# I Do

When life gets busy, time passes faster than a summer thunderstorm. Sarah watched her family growing up before her very eyes. Often she wished Michael could see the results of what they had brought into this world together.

In 1861, Mary who had been away for several years, announced her pending marriage to Horace. The ceremony, again held in the parlor, was far more traditional than when Nancy and Henry were wed. Conrad also met a wonderful girl and fell in love. When, in 1863, the two were joined in marriage, Sarah watched him and tried to hide her inner sadness as he packed his few belongings and left to begin a new life with his own wife. George met an untimely death in 1862 at the tender age of twenty.

Of the children who remained at home, the two eldest, Simon and Lavina, were like sturdy rocks, standing by their mother through all the ups and downs. Each spring Simon planted anew with the help of his younger brothers,

167

William, Herman and Jacob. He had been taught well at the hands of his father.

Still young at heart, Sarah did her best to maintain the home and the land she and Michael had settled in 1854. That seemed like a lifetime ago. When her longtime friend, Fred Frank, lost his wife, Nancy, she was there for him to listen to his woes and remind him of the good times and accomplishments he and Nancy had experienced.

*　　　*　　　*

Jessie yawned and stretched out on the floor, warm and cozy, her eyelids heavy with a sudden need for sleep. "What a story. I must say, I never expected this," She waved one hand around to suggest the nature of 'this'. ". . . when we came in from the rain."

Rosie was leaning against one wall. Her brown eyes twinkled as she cocked her head and teased Jessie. "How you gonna write this story, Miss Reporter? Ya gotta hope the readers aren't as skeptical as you are."

Arthur actually laughed when Jessie stuck her tongue out at Rosie. "Looks like you two are ready to settle in for the night. Let me tell you just one more little story before you go to sleep."

"Sure, why not? What's it about?"

"Well, it's about a little situation that began to develop between Sarah and her neighbor, Fred Frank.

"Following Nancy's death, Sarah tried to look in on Fred every few weeks to be sure he was still okay. Simon would hitch up the horse and join her when she would decide to deliver a warm loaf of bread just out of the oven or a slice of fruit pie rescued from the grip of her children. It made her happy to be able to make the gesture.

"In return, Fred was sometimes seen to converse with one or more of the boys on his way to or from Springville. They shared their concerns about the work to be done and welcomed his advice. Always, they relayed the details of their brief conversations with the rest of the family when gathered at dinnertime.

"This casual friendship had been going on for several years. Then, one morning, Fred paid Sarah a visit."

\*       \*       \*

Fred showed up after the older children were off somewhere carrying out the day's activities and the younger ones were at school. Inviting him in, Sarah found a mug, poured some coffee for both, then sat down.

Sarah watched Fred as he sat there. He appeared deep in thought as he fingered the lip of the mug she had provided. He was absorbed, at least for the moment, in watching a single thread of steam rise out of the fresh brewed coffee. He shifted, somewhat uneasy, and looked across the table at her.

"Sarah, we been neighbors for goin' on ten years now. You 'nd Nancy was mighty good friends until she up 'nd died. I been thinkin' - - -

169

He picked up his mug and took a slow draught of the hot coffee, holding the liquid for a moment behind closed lips before he swallowed. Again, he looked at Sarah. "Like I said, I been thinkin, . . . Michael died, what, three years ago last Friday? All yer older children are gone off 'nd got themselves married –'nd ya lost George. Most what ya got left is all yer youngins. Well, I ain't sayin' ya can't handle it 'cause I know ya can, but, well, I been thinkin'."

Sarah reached across the table and placed a hand on Fred's weather-beaten arm.

"Go ahead, Fred. Tell me what you've been thinking."

"Well, Sarah, I know I'm a bunch older'n you, 'nd I can see by lookin' at ya that ya got a hunk o' life left in ya yet. So, I was wonderin' if . . if ya might consider marryin' me."

Fred suddenly lost what little nerve he had gathered in order to face her in the first place. She watched his eyes dart off to some point beyond her in the corner of the room. She was amused by Fred's obvious discomfort and a big smile lit her face as she turned to see what he might be looking at.

"Are you checking to see if I keep a clean house?"

Fred looked back at her. "Aw, now I . . . "

"I'm just teasing you, Fred, just teasing."

Sarah realized he had again brought his attention back to her. This time, she was flustered and she lowered her eyes so as not to look at him.

"What do ya have ta say, Sarah? Will you marry me? I might not be much ta look at, but I promise ta take good care o' you 'nd yer youngins."

Sarah thought about the wonderful life she had with Michael. She thought about his twelve children. Now, one by one, they were leaving her nest. *Mary was the first to go. It seems so long ago. Now she has little ones of her own. Then there was Nancy's wedding; makes me want to smile. Michael died not long before Catherine's wedding; so sad. Conrad was the first son to go. Then there was poor George.* How she missed them all.

Sarah's eyes refocused on Fred and she realized she had just gone on her own personal journey and left him out. *Fred's a nice man. I certainly know him well enough to trust his intentions, and he does get along fine with the children.*

Again, she looked at Fred.

"Yes, Fred. I will marry you. I have little enough to offer, but I think we'll do just fine together." She smiled and blushed, and being forty-five years old, wondered why she was blushing.

# Time To Leave

Arthur looked down at the two sleeping girls. There they were, breathing peacefully after a long day of travel, trouble and tales. It was nice to have someone to watch, to have someone to protect from the cold wetness of the April rain. He sighed, a long quiet sigh so as not to disturb them. And somewhere (no one knows where or how) he smiled.

It was a tender smile, the kind that forms when one is remembering the good times. The smile broadened as he mentally ticked off the names of all the children who had grown up under his care. There were so many.

Of course, there were Michael and Sarah's twelve kids. Mary, eighteen when they first arrived, was hardly a child. But Arthur still loved her. She had played such an important role when Jacob, the first to be born under his roof, was just a baby. Catherine and Nancy were giddy teenagers when the family arrived. But, like most, they grew into responsible young women before leaving the nest. Then there were the three oldest boys – Simon,

172

George and Conrad. Right off the bat, those three had borne huge responsibilities for children their age. Michael surely would not have been as successful without them.

Eight-year-old Lavina was just old enough to become Jacob's "little mother" following his birth in 1854. She followed Mary around like a trained kitten, wanting to prove her worth to elder sister and to mother. Sometimes she simply drove her sister crazy.

Tiny Sarah, whose dreamy thoughts and silly ways tugged at the heartstrings of both mother and siblings, left this world far too soon. At the age of nine, she had succumbed to pneumonia, leaving her family grieving while she went to play in an eternal playground. William, her constant companion, was just two years younger and surely felt her loss the most.

Herman and Jacob, so much younger than the other three boys, brought up the rear of the family line until the birth of Louisa just a year before Michael died. Though a surprise, the baby girl gave her mother much joy and consolation in the years that followed.

Then there were all the other children of all the families that came and went over the years.

*Let me see, there were twelve . . . no, thirteen of them. Dear me, I loved them all.*

There was Burt. Then Esther and Elsie, the twins. They were fun to watch. Then Alvin and Richard. Then a family came who didn't operate the farm. They were city kids: Chris, Jerry, Robert and Ricky. They were wide-eyed and filled with wonderment at the vastness of the outdoors. Finally there were Scott and Laura.

A tear formed on one of his windows as Arthur thought about all the little children he had cared for and protected. It trickled slowly down to the old wood frame to be absorbed, once again, into the very fabric of the dwelling.

As the sun climbed over the nearby hilltop and spread across the landscape, Rosie and Jessie began to stir. Arthur watched Rosie roll onto her back and rub her beautiful brown eyes. Meanwhile, Jessie lifted her head and, propped up on her elbows, yawned a spacious yawn.

"Good morning, ladies. I hope you had a restful sleep in my humble abode."

"Well, good morning yourself," Rosie replied. "What a beautiful day this is going to be."

Groaning, Jessie climbed into a standing position and brushed herself off.

"R-i-g-h-t! This experience makes the mattress at home seem like a featherbed. Oh, my aching body!"

Arthur chuckled and watched Rosie pull two granola bars from her backpack. Then he grew silent, suddenly aware they would soon be leaving.

Jessie began moving toward the door as she stripped the paper off her breakfast.

"I'm gonna see if the car will start. Be back in a minute." And she was gone.

"Rosie?"

"Yes?"

"Do you have to go so soon?"

"Yes . . . You know it's time. Thank you for telling us about Michael and Sarah. It's amazing to learn about the life they lived and how things were back then."

For a long moment Rosie stood silent, looking out a large picture window at the ravine, at the trees that were beginning to turn green, at the signs of the new life of spring.

"Maybe someday, someone will find you and move in."

"I'd like that, Rosie. I really would."

The sound of an engine broke through their conversation. First it was a sputter, then a steady hum. A moment later, a triumphant Jessie re-entered the house. A wide grin lit up her face.

"It started. Can you beat that? It actually started. . . . Come on, Rosie. Let's get out of here. A nice hot shower is waiting for me when I get home."

Arthur remained silent while the girls gathered their things and began to leave. He knew they would never be back.

*How long,* Arthur wondered, *before someone else would come around again?*

Half way to the road, Rosie turned and offered a silent good bye as her eyes scanned the tired old building.

Arthur heard and replied.

"Tell others about me. . . . Please tell others."

*Please don't forget.*

175

# Epilogue

The September afternoon was sunny and warm. Recent crisp nights were having their effect on the trees in the yard and shades of autumn were beginning to appear. Two cars pulled to a stop in front of the house, one with a single professional looking occupant, the other with a young couple. Car doors opened and, after a brief conversation, the three approached the front door.

Arthur stood silent but alert, waiting to see the reason for their visit. No one had visited since Jessie and Rosie's departure. No one had cared.

"This place needs a lot of work," the young professional was saying, "but I think you'll like it."

Hand in hand, the couple entered, looking here and there to see what they might see.

"It's been empty for a long time, but it's well built. It's looking for someone like you to bring it back to life . . . a real fixer-upper."

During the next half hour, Arthur watched the man and woman slowly fall in love with what they found. He didn't breathe a word. He didn't even let out a sigh. Quiet as can be, he watched and waited and hoped. Finally the words he wanted to hear came in a quiet conversation held on the pathway just outside the door.

"We would like to put an offer in on the house. It's just what we want."

*"Yes – s – s – s!"*

The young couple looked back and commented on the fresh breeze that seemed to envelop the house and yard.

## The Author

Rick Iekel: Husband, father of four, grandfather of ten, is retired and writing. During a 35-year career in aviation, writing was a pastime for quiet Sunday afternoons and peaceful summer vacations. A storyteller, he maintains a lifelong fascination with real stories about real people in real places. "With real-life stories so entertaining," he muses, "why would I try to create believable fiction?" Raised on a farm in the foothills of the Allegheny Mountains, he now resides with his wife in Rochester, New York.

## Other Books
*(Available in print or electronic form at Amazon.com)*

## LIFE LINES
A Selection of Poetry Written by Helen Corrigan Iekel
*with*
*Introduction and Commentary by Rick Iekel*

## The Candles of My Life

Made in the USA
Middletown, DE
21 March 2017